THE LAST
SEDER
OF JAMES

THE LAST SEDER OF JAMES

A Journey Through Passover

Book One in the Passover Trilogy

Lon A. Wiksell, D. Min. & Ryan Wiksell

Published by Our Father Abraham
Kansas City

www.ourfatherabraham.com

ISBN: 978-1-7323705-3-1
Wiksell, Lon, 1949—
The Last Seder of James : A Journey Through Passover / Lon A. Wiksell, D.Min.

Cover design by Ryan Wiksell
Illustrations by Nathen Reynolds

OUR FATHER
Abraham

Our Father Abraham is a ministry of Lon A. Wiksell, D.Min. The organization's mission is to be a vital resource for people of all backgrounds to understand the Hebraic roots, and essential Jewishness, of the Christian faith.

Our Father Abraham accomplishes this through teaching, worship, advocacy, and celebration of the Jewish Sabbath and other festivals.

Visit our website at: **www.ourfatherabraham.com** to learn more.

For Fran -LW

For Christina -RW

May the God of Abraham, Isaac and Jacob keep you and bless you. And may you love him with all your heart, soul, and strength.

Table of Contents

INTRODUCTION

The Last Seder of James is a unique combination of historical fiction and biblical teaching. The title refers to the story portion, wherein James the brother of Jesus eats a ritual Passover meal (or *Seder*) on the night before he is martyred. The book is subtitled *A Journey Through Passover* because it is designed to impact the reader emotionally, intellectually and spiritually, through a variety of experiences. Below is a quick overview of the sections that follow, and how various readers can make the most of their journey through them.

Note: This introduction provides basic background information about the premise of the story, the characters, the setting and the festival of Passover. Some readers may choose to skip this section if the information is already familiar to them, or if they simply prefer reading fiction over nonfiction.

Following the Introduction is the Story, with a Prologue, Parts I – III, and an Epilogue. The Prologue is written in first-person memoir style. The writer identifies herself as Priscilla, known in Scripture as a valued partner to Paul, and co-missionary with her husband Aquila. In the story she is presented as a personal friend and associate of the Apostles John and James as well. Parts I – III subsequently depict, in third-person perspective, John's night-time visit to James in his prison cell, followed be an astonishing climax at the Temple. The Epilogue then returns to Priscilla's first-person perspective to close out the narrative.

After the Story section comes the Teaching. This begins with an extended commentary on the story, which provides cross-references to the scenes referred to in each commentary note. This allows the commentaries to function either as endnotes (to be referenced as needed) or as a nonfiction teaching to be read in its entirety after the story.

Next is a series of lessons about the historical and biblical significance of the Passover tradition, first to Judaism, and then to Christianity. Insight is provided as to the nature and timing of Passover, and the elements of a traditional Seder meal. In the process, the connection is made to the person and ministry of Jesus, who is the Lamb of God, and the ultimate fulfillment of Passover.

All information provided after this is for reference, including an additional teaching about the seven Levitical Festivals, a glossary of Hebrew terms, a selection of relevant Scripture passages, a list of resources for further learning, and author bios. It is the author's hope that the reader enjoys each section in his or her own way.

The Story

Church tradition maintains that James the brother of Jesus was imprisoned during Passover in AD 62. *The Last Seder of James* begins as a novel, featuring an imaginative exploration of this episode in history. The Story supposes that John the Apostle travels from his home in Ephesus to visit James in his cell, and brings a Seder meal with him, so they can celebrate Passover together. As they observe the order of the meal, various elements evoke memories of Jesus' upbringing and ministry. In the process, the two men wrestle with issues in their past, and allow the Holy Spirit to prepare their hearts for things to come.

The narrative presented here is a work of historical fiction. Its purpose is to open the eyes of the reader to the first-century context of the gospel message, and to enlighten the Church to see these events from the perspective of the time and culture upon which our faith is founded. Although the story is based on Scripture and certain historical records (of varying degrees of reliability) the authors have also exercised artistic liberties for the sake of character and dramatic development. Several aspects of the Passover celebration described here were not practiced during the life of James and John. However, due to limited knowledge of first-century Passover customs, and the aim of this work to educate a modern audience about the traditional Seder meal, certain anachronisms are inevitable.

In short, every effort has been made to honor the facts of history (as they are known) and the spiritual truths found in the Bible, while developing characters and plotlines in an engaging manner.

The Characters

James and John, the major characters in the Story, were widely regarded as two of the three pillars of the early Church. [1] Although they are each highly unique historical figures, unfortunately they bear two of the most commonplace names in the New Testament. Thus, they are subject to some confusion. The following profiles may help to distinguish them from other well-known characters, and provide some background for understanding this story.

James

Commonly identified as the Brother of Jesus, James was a son of Mary and Joseph, and therefore a half-brother to Jesus, and brother to Joseph, Simon, Judas, and their sisters. (Matthew 13:55) He should

---

[1] The third was Peter (Galatians 2:9).

not be confused with James the Son of Zebedee (brother of the John in this story), or James the son of Alphaeus, both members of the twelve disciples appointed by Jesus.

James, having grown up with Jesus, would have had a unique perspective on his character and the events of his life. Although he was likely a skeptic during Jesus' earthly ministry (John 5:7) it is clear the Resurrection changed his mind. In fact, James was transformed so completely in this process that he became the head of the Church at Jerusalem, and functioned as the chair of the momentous Jerusalem Council. [2]

For the purpose of this story, James is presumed to have been two years younger than Jesus. Since he was the first son born after Jesus, this seems a reasonable estimate. This would make him approximately sixty-three years old at the time of this story in AD 62.

James authored one book of the New Testament, the epistle commonly known as "James".

John

John son of Zebedee (John the Apostle, John the Beloved, John the Evangelist) was one of the twelve disciples appointed by Jesus. Among these twelve were the sons of Zebedee—John and his older brother James—whom Jesus called "Sons of Thunder". This John should not be confused with John the Baptist (John the Baptizer, John the Immerser) who was Jesus' cousin.

At his crucifixion, Jesus entrusted his mother's care to John, "the disciple whom Jesus loved." (John 19:25-27) John, being the youngest of the disciples, may have been just thirteen years old at the beginning of Jesus' ministry, which was generally accepted as the age for a young

---

[2] Acts 12:17, 15:13-29, 21:18-24

4

man to become a "son of the commandments" and thus be expected to keep them. Thus, at the time of Jesus' death, John may have been only sixteen, and at the time of James' death (when this story takes place) in his late forties.

John authored five books of the New Testament: the Gospel of John, the three epistles commonly known as I John, II John and III John, and the book of Revelation. Tradition holds that he died of natural causes at a relatively advanced age, while in exile on the Greek island of Patmos.

Other Characters

Several other characters are named in the Story, some of which are not developed until later in the Trilogy. Nevertheless, a brief introduction may be in order for the characters of Priscilla, Simon, Jude and Ananus.

Priscilla. The narrator for the story is known in the Bible as the wife of Aquila of Pontus and an invaluable partner in ministry to the Apostle Paul. Little else is known about her, except that she was a tent-maker by trade, she served the churches at Rome, Corinth and Ephesus (in that order), was regularly named before her husband (indicating a rare prominence among women), and that she helped mentor Apollos, a renowned teacher in the early Church. There is also a theory that she is the anonymous author of the Epistle to the Hebrews. Priscilla's character is explored in much greater detail in the second book of the Trilogy, a fifty-day fictional memoir entitled *I Am Priscilla*.

Simon. Jesus' next oldest brother after James was named Simon (or Simeon). History tells us that he succeeded his brother James as the head of the Church at Jerusalem.

Jude. Jesus' youngest brother was named Jude (or Judah, or Judas).

Very little is known about him, except that he authored the brief but powerful letter that appears at the end of the New Testament, immediately before Revelation.

Ananus. The high priest in power during Passover of AD 62 was Ananus ben Ananus (or Ananus II), known to history as the man who imprisoned James. He was deposed immediately afterward, and eventually went on to play a pivotal role in the Jewish revolt four years later.

The Setting

The physical setting for the story is a prison in Jerusalem, where James is being held prior to his execution on a charge of simply "breaking the law". The story presumes that this prison is located in the basement of the Antonia Fortress, which is adjacent to the north wall of the Temple compound.

The historical setting is Passover in the year AD 62, which is widely regarded as the "beginning of the end" for the Temple. According to some accounts, the high priest at the time, Ananus ben Ananus, was ousted as a result of his treatment of James. Some have even gone so far as to name this as a root cause of the Roman siege of Jerusalem, which took place later in the same decade.

The Passover Seder

A Passover Seder (SAY-der) is a meal that commemorates God's redemptive work in the Exodus from Egypt. Passover is the first of seven festivals outlined in God's commandments to Israel found in Leviticus chapter twenty-three.

The story of Passover is found in the book of Exodus, when God frees his people from slavery in Egypt. As a judgment on the false gods of Egypt, God sends ten plagues, the tenth of which results in the death of every firstborn male. God tells Moses that if the Israelite families each slaughter a lamb and spread the blood on the doorframes of their homes, the Angel of Death would "pass over" them, and they would be safe.

God instituted Passover so that we would always remember God's grace, mercy, love and redemptive purposes. Passover has been celebrated now for over three thousand years.

Jesus' last meal on earth, often called "The Last Supper" (recorded in the gospels of Matthew, Mark and Luke, and referred to by Paul in his first letter to the Corinthians) is widely recognized as a Passover Seder. This was the occasion in which Jesus commanded his disciples (including us) that when we eat the bread and drink the cup together, we do so in remembrance of him. Thus, every observance of Communion or Eucharist, within the Christian Church, functions as a Passover Seder in miniature.

When is Passover?

Passover comes each year in the Spring, either in March or April. It can be challenging to keep track of the date of Passover each year, because there is not a consistent relationship between the Gregorian and Hebrew calendars. The table on page 95 provides a list of upcoming dates for Passover.

Jesus and Passover

Many Bible translations refer to the last Passover meal (or Seder) of Jesus and his disciples as "The Last Supper". [3] Jesus would have celebrated this Passover meal every year of his life. Along with the six other festivals outlined in Leviticus 23, Passover provided the basic rhythm to his seasons and years. Jesus would have celebrated it first as a child with his family, then later as the head of the household, after his father presumably died. It would have been Jesus' responsibility as the eldest son to lead and provide for the family.

When Jesus began his ministry he certainly would have spent Passover with his disciples, and his last Passover meal may have been the third or fourth time he celebrated it with them. As their rabbi he would have arranged for each Passover Seder and selected the lamb, to have it sacrificed at the Temple.

Jesus would have identified deeply with the Passover lamb, knowing his life was meant to be surrendered, and his blood was meant to be shed. His blood was to be like the blood painted on the doorposts of each Hebrew dwelling in Egypt, rescuing them from death. And his blood upon us is a sign of our saving relationship with him. He knew that he was the "Lamb of God who takes away the sin of the world." (John 1:29) In the past, the law required that countless lambs be sacrificed every year at the Temple, but Jesus has fulfilled this law. He came to be our Passover Lamb forever.

The Passover Trilogy

Of the seven Jewish festivals outlined in Leviticus chapter 23, three of them carried expectations of pilgrimage. As commanded in Deuteronomy 16:16, all Jews who were able to travel to Jerusalem did so for the festivals of Passover, Shavu'ot (Pentecost) and *Sukkot*

---

[3] Matthew 26:17-30, Mark 14:12-26, Luke 22:1-23

(Tabernacles). These three are referred to as the Pilgrimage Festivals, and form the basis of the trilogy.

The Last Seder of James, as the first book, is focused on the first Pilgrimage Festival—Passover. The second book, *I Am Priscilla,* is about Pentecost, and the Counting of the Omer leading up to it. The third book, entitled *Seventy,* will feature the Feast of Tabernacles, alongside the other fall festivals (primarily Rosh Hashanah and Yom Kippur).

Although this book is the only one to feature Passover explicitly, the themes of Passover (such as Creation, Exile, Deliverance, Covenant, and Redemption) define the trilogy as a whole. The three-part narrative thus proposes that all the Jewish festivals are built upon the foundation laid by Passover. Thus the collection is known as the Passover Trilogy.

Hebrew Terms

In this edition, Hebrew terminology is kept to a minimum. Wherever Hebrew is important to the Story or the Teaching, footnotes are provided for definitions or other background information. Pronunciation guides and further explanations can be found in the Hebrew Terms section, starting on page 121.

THE STORY

AD 62

JERUSALEM

Prologue

Wednesday Night, the 13th of Nisan[4]

We shuffled patiently amongst the crowd, inching closer to the resplendent city. The dirt was hard as cobblestone beneath our feet from the myriad travelers that had gone before us, just since this morning. Any dust that might have been loose was kicked up hours ago, leaving the road clean and smooth.

The mood was loud and jovial as we approached the great gate of the Essenes, at the southwest corner of Jerusalem, but I could feel it dampened by the party walking in front of us. Ten hooded men with knotted foreheads and pursed lips, shouting in whispers back and forth. Zealots, no doubt.[5] I watched the men anxiously as they grew closer and closer to the Roman checkpoint. And then, they arrived.

"A dagger? Two daggers! Hands on your head!" A Roman soldier barked his orders, and screams erupted on every side. The leader of the group—the man with two daggers—looked frantically to his brothers, but they had all recoiled at the critical moment. Three guards disrobed him and threw him to the ground, then pinned him there with a foot on his neck. The nine other men were summarily stripped to their tunics and beaten, while the leader was kicked and jabbed mercilessly.

As the blood began to flow down the slope toward our feet, the beatings were replaced with elaborate curses in Latin, then more

---

[4] The first month of the biblical Hebrew calendar (see page 94)
[5] See "The Zealots" on page 73.

rudimentary curses in Aramaic. The soldiers confiscated over a dozen daggers and a pair of swords, then turned around and brandished them at the necks of the hapless revolutionaries.

Soon the appalling scene grew quiet. The only sound that remained was that of women and children weeping. Then I saw the leader wrestle one hand free, place it on his head and pull it away soaked in blood. His face contorted with rage and he inhaled through gritted teeth.

"Death to Rome!" the Zealot screamed. And in the blink of an eye Rome brought death to the Zealot. Impaled through the heart with his own blade. *He who lives by the sword, dies by the sword.*

Everyone saw it. That was the point.

More soldiers arrived at the gate to drag the offenders away, and we were up next.

It's late now, and I'm writing this account by candlelight. I traveled here with John the Elder (some know him as the Apostle, or the Beloved) from Ephesus to visit our brother James in prison. Five days by sea to arrive in Joppa, and a day and a half by donkey to arrive in Jerusalem.

It really was a pleasant journey for the most part. The seas were calm, and the donkeys were generally cooperative. Mostly cooperative. Part of the time. We had some rain yesterday morning, but soon the clouds parted, and the roads were dry again by mid-day. By that point the road was all uphill. We just kept climbing and climbing, and we started to feel a little sorry for our noble steeds. But as we made the final ascent, the sun was settling into the horizon behind us, lighting the city up like a torch. O Jerusalem!

I rejoiced when they said to me, "Let us go to the House of ADONAI.

*Our feet are standing in your gates, Jerusalem—Jerusalem, built as a
city joined together. There the tribes go up, the tribes of ADONAI.* [6]

For we haven't come to a mountain that can be touched, but to
Mount Zion—to the city of the living God, the heavenly Jerusalem. At
the top of the hill, overlooking the city, one can almost see into the
future—with thousands upon thousands of angels, a joyous gathering,
and the assembly of the firstborn who are written in a scroll in
heaven. And dare I say that in its light, beyond its light, in the midst of
the city, our eyes are opened to the one true God—the Judge of all! [7]

We didn't climb this hill alone. The ship—and the road—to
Jerusalem were packed to the limit. Jews from every corner of the
world. Besides myself (Priscilla), there's John and his wife Susanna,
Demetrius and his wife Thea, as well as John's student Milos. [8] (I'll
have to write more about them at another time.) Sadly, my husband
Aquila was unable to come.

We carried no swords, no daggers, and nothing to extort. Our only
valuables were an ossuary and a silver cup, and even those were
precious only to us. But that didn't make our entry to the city any less
nerve-racking. I was shaking violently as I held up my arms for a pat-
down. I shudder to think what's become of our city.

Nevertheless, we got through unscathed. Only a moment after we
made it past the guards and through the gate, we heard a shout.
"Priscilla! John! Susanna!" It was Jude—Jesus' youngest brother—
shouting each of our names in turn. Then he belted out a joyous song
of praise like he'd seen the Messiah himself on a white horse, not a

---

[6] Psalm 122. As a Song of Ascents this was traditionally sung by pilgrims to Jerusalem
on their approach to the city.

[7] See Hebrews 12:22-23. It is presumed that Priscilla is quoting this from the oral
tradition, or her own teaching, prior to the writing of Hebrews.

[8] While Priscilla, John and Demetrius are based on real biblical characters, Susanna,
Thea and Milos are entirely fictional.

15

half-dozen panicky and bedraggled donkey riders in need of a bath. The crowd stared while we hoofed the last few steps into the House of Zadok,[9] as if we were royalty. (I could hear them murmuring their disappointment when they learned otherwise.)

But the residents of the house were not disappointed at all. Jude couldn't stop hugging and kissing us. And when he did stop, his wife and children arrived to pick up where he left off. My cheeks are sore now from laughing and smiling. Even James' imprisonment couldn't prevent that.

Next Jesus' sisters and their families, and lastly Simon—next brother in line after James—and his family arrived. Simon, as one of the elders at Zadok, offered to serve as our host, and provide us whatever we needed for food and beds.

The time for the evening meal had passed, but Simon fed us anyway. Some members of our group wanted to go and visit James right away, but were told that there was already a crowd of visitors there for the evening. Arrangements are being made for us to see him tomorrow evening instead. A part of me can't wait another moment to see my dear brother. But the other part of me is falling asleep, even as I write. So I will offer this bedtime prayer.

May ADONAI bless you and keep you. May he make his face shine upon you, and be gracious to you. May he turn his face toward you and grant you shalom.[10]

---

[9] The characters enter the Essene Gate, and are welcomed into the (fictional) House of Zadok. These details refer to the theoretical connection between early Christians and members (or former members) of the Essene sect of Judaism. This is explored in greater detail in the second book of the Trilogy.

[10] Numbers 6:24-26

Thursday Night, the 14th of Nisan

Consider it all joy, my brothers, when you encounter various trials, knowing that the testing of your faith produces endurance. And let endurance have its perfect work, so that you may be perfect and complete, lacking in nothing.

But if any of you lacks wisdom, let him ask of God, who gives to all without hesitation and without reproach, and it will be given to him. But let him ask in faith, without any doubting—for one who doubts is like a wave of the sea, blown and tossed by the wind.[11]

I crossed out "wind" and wrote in "storm". But then I wondered if that was too strong for what James was trying to say. So I crossed out "storm" and wrote "wind" back in.

It's late now as I sit in my writing corner at the House of Zadok trying to translate James' beautiful Hebrew into beautiful Greek.[12] It isn't easy; Hebrew is such an artful language. Every word has such a range of meaning that's hard to capture without context. I managed to do it well enough with John's letter to the churches,[13] but when John writes in Hebrew, you can tell he's thinking in Greek as well. James, by contrast, knows almost no Greek. He's never traveled outside of Judea, Samaria and Galilee.

James is one of the dearest people in the world to me. Our lives have taken very different courses, and yet we've always understood each other.

I'm often recruited to act as a scribe. My father was a rabbi, and taught me and my sister as if we were sons, so my Hebrew and Greek

---

[11] James 1:2-6
[12] See "Translation" on page 73.
[13] Priscilla is referring here (fictitiously) to the First Epistle of John. The story supposes that it's the only one of his letters to have been written thus far.

17

are strong. But I would have come whether they needed me or not—for James. The brother of Jesus. And now leader of the community of Believers in Jerusalem. He was jailed a few weeks ago by the Sanhedrin, on what charge? *Breaking the law.* Nothing more was added. James is almost universally beloved—even by unbelievers, who call him James the Just. The outcry was swift and passionate, but the rumors are bad.

Not in their most fantastic visions could the Temple leaders hope for a reputation like that of James. Granted, he was once one of his brother's favorite skeptics, always wary and critical of his ministry. But ever since the day the risen Messiah appeared to him—even before he appeared to the Eleven—James' devotion to Jesus has been total and absolute.

Like his brother, James remained unmarried, living in a musty room in the Lower City, shunning all possessions and maintaining only a single shabby cloak to his name. As a result, his focus on the poor (in body, mind or spirit) of this city has no equal. Thousands upon thousands have been fed, healed, forgiven, freed, or reconciled. Is there even one family in Jerusalem that has been untouched by his compassion? Not one that I can imagine.

They can't keep James in prison forever. Surely the festival crowds will demand his release. Or John will proclaim this the year of the favor of ADONAI, and by his prayers the prison walls will crumble. Or the shackles will fall from James' wrists in the middle of the night. Something. Anything. *Ask in faith, without any doubting...*

The sun had fully set before we could gather round the massive dining table for a meal. It was the loudest meal of my life—and with this group, that's quite a claim. Everyone had a story or three, and they were all about James. We rejoiced over his good works, wept over his trials and laughed uproariously at his antics. (Despite James' piety, he has a razor-sharp sense of humor, and won't suffer anyone's nonsense.) But then I got a bitter chill, when I realized that we'd begun talking about him in the past tense, not the present. *One who doubts is like a wave of the sea...*

The night was frigid when I stepped outside to think and to pray. Within half an hour John and our whole party came out to tell me the meal was over, and we were going to visit James. Simon and Jude sent us ahead with their blessing—six visitors was plenty.

Even now I struggle to write it: James looks bad. His collarbone is sticking out, his beard is dry and matted, and his skin is caked with dust. I asked Simon what happened to all the food, clothing and soap his friends have sent. He doesn't think any of it is getting past the guards.

James was thrilled to see us, and smiled like a boy on holiday throughout our visit, but every time he spoke he emitted a barking cough. The sound made me want to sit down and weep.

But that wasn't the worst part. I don't think he looked at John even once. He offered him a curt "shalom" and nothing more. John stayed quiet, and seemed to be gazing intently at James the entire time. I won't pretend to be surprised by this. If I am honest, it was exactly as I'd feared. John and James have never been friends.

It puzzles me, and wounds me to the heart, I love them both so much. They would go to the gallows for one another, out of loyalty, but I don't know that they've ever shared a meal, or even a conversation. John the Elder, and James the Just. Two of the three pillars of the church, standing together, yet turning away.

Eventually a guard banged on the gate, demanding that we wrap up our visit, when James produced a roll of papers from underneath his bench, and handed it to me. He told me it was a letter to the twelve tribes of the Diaspora—to the believers all over the world—written in

19

Hebrew. He asked me to distribute it for him, first to Ephesus, then everywhere else. But first I was to translate it into Greek, and give it that *special touch* I'm apparently so famous for. Then he winked at me—shameless charmer. But I didn't argue. I was honored.

On the walk home, John led the way by himself, his shoulders drooping. I quickened my pace to catch up. I told him how obvious it was that he and James needed some time alone. He nodded politely. I suggested, on behalf of the group, that we all stay home while he visits James by himself tomorrow night. I kept talking to drown out his protests. Susanna, Thea and I would spend the day tomorrow gathering some food and drink for him to smuggle in his cloak. It would have to be at night, because the daytime guards are too strict. But even the night watchmen would need money to turn a blind eye. So we'll make sure John has enough. And also a proper disguise to make sure he could go unrecognized. And dinner ready at home for when he returned. Everything I could think of to say.

Eventually, John stopped walking. He looked up at the night sky, resplendent with stars.

"Are you meddling again, Priscilla?"

"Maybe."

"Hm." John nodded thoughtfully. I felt my cheeks burning.

"I just can't take another day of it, John. That silent grudge. It makes me want to jump out of my skin."

"It's late," he said cryptically. He turned his eyes back to the stars, then looked at me again. Though I got the feeling he was looking at my chin instead of my eyes. "I just have one condition, dear Lady."

"Anything."

"What you say is true. I need to do go alone. You cannot come with me, so there will be no one to record our time together. But I will remember what we say and repeat it all for you when I return."

"Yes, of course, John. I'm honored."

"And I will need everything you can gather for me, thank you. I need to go prepared." He narrowed his eyes and smiled knowingly. "It is the first night of Passover, is it not?"

PART I

"Did you bring my mother?"

"James—"

A hacking cough echoed against the barren walls, followed by a distant barrage of curses. It was hard to think. The cough escalated, as did the epithets, until a *thump* and a *crunch* restored a type of peace to the subterranean tangle of holding cells.

"Your mother died in Ephesus, years ago," [14]

A thick silence ensued while James stared at his wringing hands. He could feel the prison grit covering his skin, but could barely see it in the darkness of his cell. By the dim light of the torch in the stone corridor he could just make out John's silhouette standing in the aperture. He groaned painfully before speaking again.

"I know."

"I left her ossuary with Simon. We're looking for a suitable place for it," John said. "A permanent place."

"Oh. Good." James grunted, looking up briefly. As John's eyes adjusted, the moment afforded him a glance at the fresh wounds on James' face. His lips were distorted, and one eye was badly swollen.

"I had to remove it under cover of darkness. The Ephesian church is proud to be known as her final resting place, but her bones belong here. In Jerusalem. We'll have to break it to them gently." James nodded gravely, and John stood in silence for a moment. "She died peacefully, of old age. She spoke of you often."

"And now she's gone. But you—you came here alone?" James raised his brow and leaned over, as if to discover someone hiding behind John.

---

[14] See "James' Late Mother" on page 74.

"It's just me."

"So it would seem."

"James, I—"

"Do you know how many visitors I've had, in the weeks since they brought me here? Most nights it was a constant stream, to the point the guards found it bothersome. But nobody knew I was being executed tomorrow, till this morning, when they told me. You didn't know either, did you?"

"No. Wait—"

"So here I am, my last night on Earth, with just one visitor. It could have been so many people—friends, relatives, dignitaries—but it had to be John, son of Zebedee. It had to be the man who took my place in my brother's heart."

"You mean your mother's heart?"

James shook his head irritably. "Yes. My mother."

John took a step forward, and hesitated. "I'm sorry. I never meant to supplant you."

"Sit down, John. You've came a long way; I assume you're going to tell me the reason." James glared at the makeshift bench bolted to the opposite wall, but it remained empty. Instead, he felt the sensation of cold metal touching his weather-beaten hands.

"She wanted me to give you this," John said, in little more than a whisper. "It was your father's."

James startled, the hardness melting from his face in an instant. "I know this cup." [15]

"When he died, he passed it to your brother. When your brother—" John paused respectfully, "When your brother departed, it went back to your mother. She made me promise to put it directly into

---

[15] See "James' Cup" on page 75.

your hands."

The cup was recently polished, and glinted subtly but playfully in the torchlight, out of place like a diamond ring on a corpse. James held it gingerly, turning and tilting it, feeling the patterns and textures on its side, and running his finger along the rim.

"She was proud of you, James."

"Mother—" James tenderly pressed the silver goblet to his chest and closed his eyes. He rocked gently back and forth, continuing to mutter what could have been a blessing, a lament, or both. Soon his body came to rest and he opened his eyes.

"I also brought wine and *matzah*," [16] John whispered, leaning in close. "And the rest."

"You brought a Seder?" [17] James asked abruptly.

"Shh." The left corner of John's lips turned upward ever so slightly as he re-seated himself on the floor in the middle of the cell. "This is Passover, is it not?"

John's hands worked quickly in the borrowed light from the corridor. He removed one item after another from his robe and set them down in his own shadow on the floor. He was afraid of the guard; his bribe had been meager.

Within moments James could dimly make out the shank bone of a lamb, a sprig of parsley, a pouch of *matzah,* two bowls of water, a small earthen jar, a skin of wine and a candle.

"I had to cut some corners," John confessed. "We couldn't find a second candle. And the *maror* [18] and *charoset* [19] are in the same jar. Hopefully they didn't mix too much."

---

[16] Unleavened bread. Plural: *matzot* (see page 100)
[17] Ceremonial Passover meal (see page 97)
[18] Bitter herbs, such as horseradish (see page 105)
[19] Chopped apple salad with nuts and honey (see page 105)

"Bitter and sweet, together? Sounds about right. It might even taste good," James quipped darkly.

John ignored him and began the traditional blessing, normally given by the woman of the house. "Blessed are you, ADONAI our God, King of the Universe..." he chanted at a whisper as he lit the candle before him and twisted it into a crack in the floor. He covered his face with his hands and completed the blessing. "...who sanctifies us with his commandments, and allows us to kindle the Passover lights— light. May it remind us of Jesus our Messiah, the Light of the World."

The effect was dim, but substantial. They could now see clearly before them the makings of a Passover Seder, arranged in orderly fashion. It struck James that this was to be his last meal. So like the final supper of his Messiah. And yet, so different.

"Would you bless the first cup, James?"

"You can do it."

John poured a careful amount of wine from the skin into the gleaming silver cup. [20] "With this, the cup of Sanctification, we remember God's promise: 'I will bring you out from under the burden of the Egyptians.'" James groaned softly and glanced around him, wondering if God might have anything similar in mind for his own situation.

John continued. "Blessed are you, ADONAI our God King of the Universe, who creates the fruit of the vine, who has kept us alive and sustained us, and brought us to this special time." John took a tiny sip from the cup and handed it reverently to James, who drained it in a moment. John glanced over his shoulder nervously to check for the guard. Seeing no one, he recited another blessing, over the washing of hands, and placed a bowl in front of John. [21]

---

[20] See "1. Drinking the Cup of Sanctification" on page 99.
[21] See "2. Washing of the Hands" on page 99.

"I wish I'd brought more water. I forgot how dirty these places are."

"It's not your fault," James chuckled wryly. "I demanded a room with a *mikveh*, [22] but the hospitality here is terrible. I don't think I'll come back."

"That's funny."

James looked down and closed his eyes, his face flushed. "Forgive me. I don't mean to be cynical." He felt a hand on his shoulder. Then he felt another hand taking off his sandals.

"John, please—"

"No, James. This is how we do it. You know that." John held the bowl while James dipped his fingers into it, then John poured a little water into both his hands and gently rubbed James' feet. The cleansing effect was negligible, but the sensation was exhilarating. James breathed deeply through his nose. He'd forgotten how large his lungs were.

John put the sandals back on James' feet, and placed the soiled water bowl to the side. He then moved the second bowl in between them. This one contained saltwater, for dipping vegetables. [23]

"At least the parsley gets a *mikveh*," John winked at his companion as he lowered the sprig into the bowl. James snorted in surprise at the joke, then took his own piece and dipped it in the water.

"I hate to admit it, but this my favorite part." James lifted his face and dropped the parsley reverently into his mouth. "Mmmm. John, do you remember the *mikva'ot* at the Temple?"

"Quite well. I was there last year."

"Did you ever feel cleaner in your life? I'm trying to remember what a cleansing feels like. Now I'm not sure I remember what color

---

[22] Bath or basin for ritual cleanliness (see page 76). Plural: *mikva'ot*

[23] See "3. Dipping the Green Vegetable *(Karpas)*" on page 99.

my skin is; even when there's some light in here I can't really tell anymore."

"No, you're right. It's marvelous—with the Temple priests there to declare you clean. I know it's the *old system,* but it still feels the same. I remember as a little boy, immersing with my father and brother; it was such an invigorating sensation. As if God himself was scrubbing the world off my skin."

James closed his eyes and sighed heavily. "I wonder what's going to happen to the Temple now. My brother was signaling its demise since the first time he visited, when I was ten years old. Of course, he couldn't come right out and say it then, like he did during his ministry. But it was pretty clear to everyone who was paying attention."

"You were there when Jesus visited the Temple as a boy."

"Sure."

"When he asked the rabbis and priests all those profound questions."

"I'm *still* grappling with those questions. The rabbis and priests probably are too."

"And when you accidentally left him behind."

"It was a big group! There were probably forty or fifty of us traveling together. I hate to say I'm not my brother's keeper, but—"

John waved off the defensive reflex. "Just tell me what it was like! Jesus and I were pretty close when he was thirty, but he never talked about his childhood. I want to hear about those Passovers in Jerusalem when you were boys."

James frowned, and John pulled out the first piece of *matzah.* [24] It was flat and oddly shaped, with a rich golden hue and rounded

---

[24] Unleavened bread

corners. He suggested they continue the Seder while they conversed, since God only knew how much time they would have.

He broke the bread in half, and wrapped the larger half in a napkin, then hid it in his robe. "The *Afikoman*" [25] he reminded James, unnecessarily. Then he recited the blessing over the smaller half. He broke that piece in half again and shared it with James, who repeated the blessing. James took a bite before speaking again.

"Of course we traveled to Jerusalem at least twice a year. Every year, even when I was riding in a sling on Mother's back. We went in the fall for *Sukkot,* [26] and in the spring for Passover. Then we would stay with family in Bethlehem during the Counting of the *Omer,* so we could easily be in the city again for *Shavuot.* [27]

"When the weather was good and everyone was healthy we could walk the Jordan valley road in six days—between Sabbaths. [28] That adds up to four weeks a year, but in truth I feel like half my childhood was spent on that rocky trail. It doesn't seem far now, but for little legs it was a lot of walking."

James took another bite of *matzah.* "You know, the journey was a festival in itself. Most of Galilee went together—you could see the caravan stretching to the horizon in both directions—singing songs, chatting loudly, mothers shouting at sons to stay on the road. The trip would start off joyfully, but halfway through, when we passed by Samaria, [29] things would get a little dour. We couldn't cross to the King's Highway on the eastern bank, so we had to skirt along the edge

---

[25] *Afikoman* is a Passover ritual involving three sheets of *matzah.* (see page 100)
[26] The eight-day long Feast of Tabernacles, the seventh of God's appointed times, as outlined in Leviticus 23. (see page 76)
[27] The Feast of Weeks, or Pentecost. This holiday occurs the day after seven weeks (fifty days) following Passover. This fifty days is called the Counting of the *Omer.*
[28] About 100 miles.
[29] See "Samaria" on page 77.

of Samaritan territory, and it made everyone feel uneasy. Plus by that point all our feet were sore and the bread was starting to get stale.

"But that final day of travel, that was a different story altogether. The moment we left the Jericho road and started uphill, everyone's mood changed. We forgot about our aching feet and our stale bread and we sang the Songs of Ascent, [30] together as one, from the marrow of our bones.

"I will lift up my eyes to the mountains—from where does my help come? My help comes from ADONAI, Maker of heaven and earth," [31] James sang quietly. "I rejoiced when they said unto me, 'Let us go to the House of ADONAI.' Behold how good and how pleasant it is for brothers to dwell together in unity!" [32]

James resumed his recollection. "We walked up and up with the city in our sights—you know Jerusalem might as well be on top of a mountain, coming from Jericho—but nobody complained. We just repeated those marvelous songs till even the birds could join us. When the Temple appeared on the southern horizon everyone stopped in their tracks and pointed. Songs were replaced with shouts of joy. Every journey, it was like seeing it for the first time. I would always grab Jesus by the shoulders and ask him what he thought. He would smile pleasantly at me, but he never replied. He just looked at it; I couldn't read his face at all."

John nodded happily throughout the story. All the information was familiar to him, but he loved the way James told it. To think that Jesus—the *boy* Jesus—was always right there with him. Except that one year, when he wasn't. James went on to describe their entrance through the Damascus Gate, and the opening rituals of the Passover

---

[30] See "Songs of Ascent" on page 78.

[31] Psalm 121:1

[32] Psalm 133:1

celebration.

"Father rarely talked, but he was always teaching. By the time I was seven or eight he took Jesus and me with him to pick out our family's Passover lamb. He had a craftsman's eye for his work, and he brought it with him to the marketplace. He couldn't afford one by himself, but his brothers trusted him to pick one out for all of us, because he was so discriminating. [33]

"Whenever we approached a lamb's booth, the vendor would stand a little taller. They all knew him, and some would even wave him on if they knew their specimens wouldn't hold up. They were all perfect, yes. But some were more perfect than others.

"It made him so happy, John. There were times I wondered if he passed over an ideal specimen just so it didn't have to end." James chuckled quietly to himself.

"He would walk up to a pen with forty or fifty lambs in it, and scan them carefully. Father held us in front of him so we could see everything he was doing. He mingled among the lambs, examining them each in turn, showing us any tiny scrapes, bruises, bad teeth, odd hair growth or even freckles.

"He never explained his reasoning, but we knew. He would sometimes tolerate tiny blemishes in the wood or stone he used in his work, but this was different. This lamb had to serve as a symbol of our freedom from bondage in Egypt, and our reconciliation to God. If we were perfect, we wouldn't need it. But we weren't, so the lamb had to be perfect instead. It took hours to find the right lamb, but if it wasn't the best lamb we could get, why even bother?"

John nodded thoughtfully. "When did Jesus start selecting the lamb himself?"

---

[33] Exodus 12:3

"It's funny you'd ask that, because I noticed something that year when Jesus was twelve. Father talked more, and mostly to him. Instead of just pointing out the flaws, he would ask Jesus to look at the gums, and the base of the tail. Afterward, I realized he was coaching him through it, so he could take over. Just like he'd been teaching him to take up his work back at home."

"It's incredible to think of Jesus himself—our Passover Lamb— selecting a Passover lamb," John interjected.

"Obviously Jesus was a really good kid. He was obedient, you know. Which is probably why nobody felt the need to supervise him," James recalled. "That year when he stayed behind, we all just assumed he'd be right there with us. Every year after that, he seemed a little more distant. Kind and helpful to all of us, of course, but you know— separate. I never really knew what he was doing."

"Where did you eat your Seder meals while you were in the city?" John asked.

"At Zechariah and Elizabeth's house."

"That's right; of course you did. Was John there too?"

"Sure, always. That was the best part. Even better than the Temple, God forgive me."

John put the remaining matzah back in the pouch, and reached for the wineskin. James continued.

"Everybody loved John. The Baptizer. [34] Jesus was courteous, and helpful. And a great listener. You could always count on Jesus, but John was a wild card. A prankster, even."

"A prankster? It's strange to hear you say it, but I suppose it makes sense. I wish I'd known him better."

"So do I. But you know he and Jesus were really close. They were

---

[34] See "John the Baptizer" on page 79.

only six months apart, after all. We called them the Cousin Twins, because they looked a bit alike, but they were completely different. John was Judean, Jesus was Galilean. John was rich, Jesus was poor. John was a talker and Jesus was a thinker. It's probably why they got along so well."

"Oh! I almost forgot about this." James glanced upward, his eyes searching the ceiling as if the words he needed were written there. "Let me tell you how wild John was, even as a kid. One time when he was fourteen, I think, he snuck out in the middle of a Seder. Then when it was time to fling open the door and welcome Elijah, [35] there was John, wearing a ridiculous smile and a camel hair beard. Elizabeth nearly jumped out of her skin."

"What? I never heard about that. What did Jesus think?"

"He laughed at first. All the kids did, but the adults were livid. I remember Jesus' reaction perfectly—after chuckling for a moment, he got quiet. While everyone else was yelling at John, Jesus got up and squeezed his arm, then nodded and gave him sort of a knowing look. Without saying a word—like an old man would do. Everyone was completely baffled."

"That must have been hard for Zechariah. Did he ever tell you the story of John's birth?"

"Every year," James said reflexively. "John usually asked Jesus to take a walk with him whenever his birth story came up. I guess he was a little embarrassed about being a 'miracle' baby. And Jesus could relate."

John rolled his eyes. "You say 'miracle' sarcastically."

"No no, I believe it. And so did they. But they didn't like hearing about it all the time, I gathered." James picked up the empty goblet

---

[35] See "Elijah" on page 80.

34

and held it next to the candle, turning it back and forth to give light to the intricate patterns encircling the rim.

"The rest of us, on the other hand—we never got tired of hearing it. You could see it on the face of every little boy and girl in that house, lip-syncing Zechariah's story from beginning to end. He never left anything out, and he never changed a single word. [36] I could still tell it exactly as he did if I wanted to. Down to his gestures."

"After Zechariah told his son's story, did Joseph follow with the story of Jesus' birth?"

"No, Father didn't think of himself as a storyteller. He was just a laborer, he would always say. When I was very young, he would insert a few details as Zechariah told it, but after a while he didn't need to anymore. And then by the time I was fifteen, you know—"

"That's right. Forgive me, James."

"It's ok. He'd been sick for a few years. And Jesus was seventeen by that time, so he stepped in and kept us all fed. [37] It worked out." James shrugged and gazed off to his left, but there was nothing to look at.

"Wasn't the Baptizer born during Passover?" John asked.

"That's right." James chuckled quietly. "I haven't thought about this for years. But now that you mention it, I remember overhearing something funny that Elizabeth told my sister. She said she went into labor with John *during* the Seder. Not only that, her birth pains started the moment they opened the door for Elijah."

"That's… that's something." John fidgeted in place at the mention of labor and birth pains, having never heard anyone talk about it openly before.

"He was definitely a Seder baby," James said. "I'll bet it's every Temple Priest's dream to have a son during Passover. By that token

---

[36] See "Oral Tradition" on page 81.
[37] See "Death of Joseph" on page 81.

John was a dream come true for Zechariah. But everything else about him seemed like a burden. He wasn't disobedient or anything. He was just—different. Eccentric.

"It's one of the reasons those crowds always followed him down to the Jordan. Most went to repent and be baptized, yes. But many were there just to see what he would do next. Naturally, the big one was when he declared Jesus 'the Lamb of God who takes away the sin of the world.' That shocked everyone. Even Jesus seemed surprised to hear it spoken out loud."

"I know Jesus tried pretty hard to keep that quiet, early on," John interjected. Mother made it difficult for him, though, at the wedding in Cana," James mused with a half-smile.

"That was before my time, too," John replied. "Just barely."

"What a scene," James leaned back against the wall behind him and gazed at the ceiling. "It was a month and a half after his baptism, and just two days after the Baptizer's latest pronouncement. Word of what had happened at the Jordan forty days prior was still buzzing around the region, and everyone was wondering where Jesus had disappeared to. Then a rumor surfaced that he was planning to attend our cousin's wedding in Cana. So of course half of Galilee showed up at the wedding, and the host was completely overwhelmed. The week's supply of wine ran out on the first day.

"I saw Mother's face when she realized what was going on. I think she felt bad for the host. I even wondered if she felt responsible—she may have even been the one who put the word out—because Mother was the one who urged Jesus to do something. And you know what happened next."

"He turned six huge jars of water into wine."

"It was his first public miracle. After that a lot of people believed that he was the chosen one of ADONAI. But not me."

Suddenly a deafening slam rocked their little cell. Their conversation died, along with all other sounds in the prison, as the family of inmates pricked their ears for clues to the disturbance. A desperate sob emerged from an unidentifiable source, followed by a blubbering plea for mercy. Slam! The sound came again, and the pleading ceased.

James and John jolted around to face the door of the cell. They sat for a moment like statues with widened eyes, ready to witness some horrible atrocity. But the chaos waned, and slowly the groans, coughs and feeble complaints resumed.

"We should get on with it." James remarked, his voice shaking. *I may be next.*

John nodded, and filled the cup a second time. Then he set it down and proceeded with the order.

Next came the Story of Deliverance, in which John recounted—in the briefest way he could—the story of Moses as a baby in the Nile, as a murderer on the run, as a shepherd encountering the voice of God, and so on. Nine times the Almighty put terrible wonders in his hands, each of which should have been more than enough to sway a nation, but nine times Pharaoh's heart was hardened. And on the night of the tenth wonder—the death of the firstborn—the occasion found its name. Passover. [38]

For the first nine plagues, the Hebrews had been exempted on the basis of their bloodline. But this night was different. The blood of another would be required—the blood of a lamb. [39] The tenth plague required a test of faith. Sacrifice a lamb and paint its blood on the doorposts of your house, and your family will be rescued from the Angel of Death. Whosoever believes shall not perish, but live.

---

[38] See "5a. The Ten Plagues" on page 101.
[39] See "5c. The Passover Lamb" on page 102.

With that, the Children of Israel were free. They left the land of their bondage loaded up with the riches they'd helped produce but never enjoyed. And they followed Moses into the wilderness, all the way to the impassable shores of the Red Sea. [40] This dead end would have been crisis enough, even if Pharaoh had not sent his army charging after. But God parted the waters before them—using the same miracle to give the Hebrews their start, and the stubborn Egyptian army its watery end.

"So began our journey from slavery to freedom, from sadness to joy, from being strangers in Egypt to becoming a great nation. The crossing of the sea represented the birth of a new nation, redeemed by the blood of a lamb, on its way to receive revelation at Sinai. God delivered his people to reveal himself to them as their Father.

"Mah nishtanah ha'lailah hazeh..." John chanted. On all other nights we do this, why on this night do we do that? All nights are good, why is this night special? [41]

"Though we are free now, we were once slaves. Not our forefathers. Not our fathers. But us. To this very day we owe our freedom to the burning bush, to the plagues, to the parting of the waters. We were slaves, but God has set us free."

"And some of us have become slaves again." James murmured.

With the story completed, John quietly began to sing. "Had he brought us out of Egypt, but not given us the Torah, [42] it would have been enough. *Dayenu!*" [43]

It felt bizarre to sing *Dayenu*, a song of praise and celebration, in nervous whispers. But sing they did, together in unison through

---

[40] See "The Red Sea" on page 81.
[41] See "5b. The Four Questions & Answers" on page 102.
[42] The Law of Moses, or Pentateuch; the first five books of the Bible.
[43] "It would have been enough" (see page 103.)

fifteen verses. From the Exodus to the Torah to the Promised Land. Each gift of God to his children, from the very beginning till now, has been a pure act of grace on our behalf. Shame on us if any step in the story of Redemption is taken for granted. No matter how much ADONAI gives us, or withholds from us, it's always enough. Whether a garden paradise, or a prison cell, his grace is sufficient. Enough. *Dayenu.*

John lifted the half-full cup he'd been holding, and recited the blessing. "With this, the Cup of Deliverance, [44] we remember God's promise: 'I will deliver you from slavery.'" He took a sip and handed it to James, who took a bigger sip.

"So what do you know about Jesus' birth?" John asked.

"Nothing, really. Mother wouldn't talk to us about it."

"Honestly? I've heard it told a hundred times," John replied.

James stared back, eyebrows raised. "Is that so?"

"Sure. She told everyone in Ephesus who would listen. The community welcomed thousands of new believers from her audience alone. I just wondered if you could add anything new."

"Well, I can't. To be honest, it sounds like you know more about my family than I do. You might as well tell *me* the story."

"Are you sure? You don't seem like—"

"John!" James interrupted, with an exasperated tone. He hung his head between his knees and drew a deep breath. Then another. "Please—forgive me. It's this place. I—I barely recognize myself." He closed his eyes and repeated one phrase over and over. "I will rejoice in many trials. Rejoice in many trials." [45] He inhaled again through his nose, then exhaled at length through his mouth. When he spoke again, it came out in a gravelly whisper. "Do you know what you are

---

[44] See "5e. The Cup of Deliverance" on page 104.
[45] James 1:2

39

to me, John?"

"I don't think so."

James looked up to meet John's uncertain gaze. "Do you know why we never worked together? Why we never quite got along?" John was silent. He could see something new was brewing in James' heart. "You know I was a cynical man once, before Jesus changed me. He made me a man of peace and trust. I grew into something I could scarcely have recognized in my youth. I had a purpose; I had followers. I held my tongue. I loved my enemies. I made peace with everyone. Everyone except you. [46]

"I thought I had come to accept this prison cell, and the fate that awaits me. I had been praying—this very evening—for readiness, for a peace that passes understanding. I thought I was prepared to give my life, like my brother did. But then you walked in the door, and everything my soul had gained flew out the window. If I had a window."

James caught his breath again and gestured aggressively. "You were the one who took my place amongst the Twelve. You followed him, and I didn't. You reclined against his chest the night before he was crucified, and I didn't. That was always *my place,* as a boy, but when it really mattered, it wasn't me. It was you. When it was time to hand Mother's care to the next in line, he didn't give her to me, he gave her to you. I was on the outside, looking in. You were *everything* I was supposed to be."

John was frozen in place, not sure how to receive the onslaught. Was it a confession, or an accusation? James paused for a moment that felt like an eternity, and spoke again.

"That's what you've always been to me, John. The thorn in my

---

[46] For more on the imagined relationship between James and John, see "James' Late Mother" on page 74.

side. The one problem I could never solve. No matter how big I got, no matter how much I grew in the faith, you were there, reminding me how small I really was."

"I never said—"

"You didn't have to say it. You didn't even have to be present. Just knowing you existed was enough. John, I'm—" James dried his face with his sleeve, and shuddered as if a chill breeze had blown through the drafty cell. He drew a long, thin breath and blew it out through battered lips. "I'm so sorry."

John moved the Seder elements to one side, and closed the gap between them. He put his hand at the side of James' neck, inviting his gaze upward to meet his own.

"My dear brother. You have done me no harm in the world. And Jesus has already completed his work in you. What more is there, except to receive the forgiveness he's already offered?" John stroked his beard slowly. "As your mother would always say, God has mercy on those who fear him." [47]

James blinked hard. At length, he looked up. "As my mother would say, every time she told the story of my brother's birth?"

"You know I don't have to—"

"Please do, John. Tell the story."

John sat silent for an extra moment. He bent down and put his face almost to the floor, then looked up into James' fragile countenance.

"It wasn't easy for her, at first," John muttered. "She felt like she'd let her son down, and didn't follow him the way she should have during his ministry. [48] For the first month in Ephesus all she could repeat in public was her annunciation prayer, 'My soul proclaims the

---

[47] Luke 1:50
[48] See "Mary" on page 83.

greatness of ADONAI, my spirit rejoices in God my Savior,' [49] and so on, like a confession. But one day she told me she felt forgiven, and the rest came out, little by little.

"Early on, it was just the story of the announcement—the angel Gabriel telling her not to be afraid, because she had found favor with God. 'Behold, you will become pregnant and give birth to a son,' he told her, 'and you shall call his name Jesus. He will be great and will be called Son of the Most High God. ADONAI will give him the throne of David, his father. He shall reign over the house of Jacob for all eternity, and his Kingdom will be without end.' [50]

"Soon she was adding the angelic visitation to Joseph. After some time she was able to recall more details of the journey to Jerusalem for the Feast of Tabernacles. She always thanked God for the kindness of Joseph's relatives in Bethlehem, who shared their *Sukkah* with them for his birth, on the first night of *Sukkot.* [51]

"You know, Luke was with us in Ephesus, before he left to join Paul on his journeys. Naturally he recorded every word of Mary's story. Our friend Theophilus [52] is trying to get him to edit all his records of Jesus and Paul together into a scroll we can distribute to the churches. I'm certain he'll do it eventually."

James was getting impatient. "Sure, but you were saying—"

"Yes, sorry. After just a few months in Ephesus, Mary was able to tell the entire story, including the choir of angels. That was her favorite part, to describe how the host of heaven appeared and the glory of ADONAI shone all around them. 'Glory to God in the highest, and on earth *shalom* to men of good will.' Your mother would sing

---

[49] Luke 1:46
[50] Luke 1:30-31
[51] See "Sukkot" on page 83.
[52] Luke 1:3

the song to us every time she told the story. Think of it—the song of *angels.*" Later she began recounting the threats from Herod, and the Magi's arrival from the east. In time she also told of the sudden flight to Egypt."

"Where I was born."

"That's right, you were." John paused for a moment to process the information. "That's interesting; every year at this time you celebrate our people's flight *from* Egypt, but you and your family fled *to* Egypt for safety, didn't you?"

"I suppose so, yes." Just then a large charcoal-gray rat scurried in to examine their meal. James took off his sandal and batted it away with hardly a look. John blanched a moment, then shook his head and recovered himself.

"It wasn't long before Mary was adding other details to her story, like the part about Jesus' circumcision on the Eighth Day, [53] and later at the time of her purification, when Simeon blessed God. Next it was the prophetess Anna at the Temple, who spoke about Jesus and the redemption of Jerusalem."

"I remember Simeon," James said. "Or I remember hearing his prayer, anyway. They say that moment was *decades* in the making for him." James closed his eyes. The muscles of his face relaxed as he recalled the sacred words. "Behold, you now have set your servant free, to go in peace as you have promised. For these eyes of mine have seen the Messiah, which you have prepared for all the world to see. A light to enlighten the nations, and glory to your people Israel." [54]

---

[53] The eighth day of Sukkot is celebrated as a separate holiday of its own, called *Shemini Atzeret* (which means "the eighth day assembly".) This supports the theory that Jesus was born on the first night of Sukkot, since his circumcision (Luke 2:21) would serve as a fulfillment of the Eighth Day festival.
[54] Luke 2:29-32

John repeated it after James, then they recited it together a third time, with faces turned toward heaven. After a moment of reverie, John lowered his eyes to see James' cheeks wet, glinting in the light of the little candle. He met John's gaze, but made no effort to excuse himself, or dry his face. Instead he allowed his eyelids to flutter, and a faint smile to cross his lips.

"These eyes have seen the Messiah," James said reverently. "They are ready to see him again."

"*Dayenu.*"

PART II

James and John sat motionless in contemplative adoration. The Spirit of God filled the dank little room, for a time transforming that harbinger of death into a place of life and abundance. The tightness and darkness that once signaled an end to all things now held the promise of a new beginning.

Death had been defeated. It occurred to James in a moment that his prison cell was not a coffin, as he had imagined. It was a womb.

With his head still bowed in worship, John spoke again, slowly and quietly. "In the sixth month of Elizabeth's pregnancy, God sent the angel Gabriel to Nazareth, a town in Galilee, to a virgin pledged to be married to a man named Joseph, a descendant of David." He looked up at James. "The virgin's name was Mary."

John proceeded to recount the entire story to the man in front of him—the second-born of Mary, but the first-born of Joseph. He listened in rapture as the plot unfolded, sitting tall and breathing deeply to absorb every detail. In time, John came to the end.

"When Joseph and Mary had done everything required by the Torah, they returned to Nazareth. And the child grew and became strong; he was filled with wisdom, and the grace of God was on him." [55] A hint of sunlight revealed itself through the door of the cell. It was almost dawn. John picked up the water bowl. "I don't think we can wash our hands with this. Not a very good Seder."

"We've done our best."

John put down the bowl and picked up another thumbnail-sized piece of *matzah,* splitting it so carefully James imagined he was dividing a diamond. "This was all I could get my hands on," John confessed..

"It's enough," James said.

---

[55] Luke 2:39-40

"We've always had enough, haven't we?" John affirmed. "Even when we didn't."

"Are you thinking of the multitude on the hillside?" James asked. "I wasn't there, you know."

"Did you know that the bread and the fish divided in our own hands that day, too?"

"Not just in his?"

"No. Like Peter walking on the water—Jesus let us in on the miracle. I had actually brought a lunch for myself," John began. "Most of Jesus' disciples did. The Twelve. The Seventy. But, of course, the crowd before us was practically starving. And while we were clutching our bags tightly and puzzling over the problem, a young boy stepped up with a smile to relinquish his little meal."

"I watched Jesus give the blessing, break the bread and the fish, and hand the pieces to us—the Twelve. So we broke them again, and handed those pieces to the Seventy, including Priscilla. We were dumbstruck for a moment as to how to proceed, until Peter remembered Priscilla's skill with numbers. So he asked her to estimate the size of the gathering.

"Priscilla gave Peter her sum: about 5,000 men, and 10,500 total. Since there were seventy disciples with food ready to distribute, she suggested the people sit down in seventy groups of one hundred fifty each. That way, each disciple only had to serve one hundred fifty men, women and children.[56]

"I kept one eye on the disciples whom I'd distributed to, waiting for them to come back and ask for more, but they never did. They just kept putting their hands back in their bags and pulling out more bread and more fish. Over and over and over. Finally the Seventy

---

[56] See "Feeding the Multitude" on page 84.

collected the leftovers and gave them to us, and each member of the Twelve ended up with a basket full."

The men sat in silence for a moment, absorbing the lesson that Jesus was always communicating to his followers. *You can do this.* Whether it was water or wine; whether it was bread, blood, or blindness, Jesus was constantly bestowing spiritual power on regular people. "It's one thing to believe in Jesus," John added. "It's another thing entirely to accept that *Jesus believes in us.*"

"It is," James replied, gesturing at the Seder between them. "Why else would we do *this*? Generations ago, our ancestors painted blood on their doorposts. God worked a miracle, but he used *our* hands to do it. And then he permitted us to renew and refresh that miracle every year. Bless ADONAI."

John nodded reverently as he picked up the little bowl of *maror* and recited the next blessing. "Blessed are you, ADONAI our God, King of the Universe, who has sanctified us with his commandments and commanded us to eat the bitter herbs." They ate together, and winced at the potency of the root. They laughed at each other as they snorted and shook their heads.

"I always take too much," James said, his eyelids fluttering.

John wiped his cheeks with the hem of his robe, composed himself and picked up the next bowl. This one contained the *charoset* [57]—to chase away the bitterness of the *maror*. He said the blessing, and the men smiled as the sweetness touched their lips. Then they consumed a few more items pulled from John's robe: two dried figs and a small cloth pouch of grilled lamb. James' last meal. [58]

When they'd scoured the pouch for every last crumb, it was time to pull out the *Afikoman*. John looked around the cell as if attempting

---

[57] Sweet apple and nut mixture. (see page 105)
[58] See "10. Eating the Meal" on page 106.

to remember where he'd "hidden" it. [59] James pointed to John's robe, and John smiled. He reached into an inside pocket, pulling out the large half of unleavened bread, from before.

"I found it. What do I win?" James joked.

"A free meal. I hope you enjoyed it."

"It was delicious, thank you."

John began the blessing over the bread. This time, however, something sounded new to James' ears.

"On the night our Messiah was betrayed, he took the *Afikoman,* and when he had blessed ADONAI, broke it"—John broke the bread in his hands—"and said, 'This is my body, given for you. Do this in remembrance of me.'" He handed a piece to James, who held it silently for a moment.

"Is that how Jesus said it?" he asked.

"Yes. Why? What do you say when you take the bread?"

"We say the same words as you, but—is that what it sounded like?"

"Yes, I remember it perfectly. And then for the wine—"

"Wait. Will you—" James put his hand over his mouth, as if to stifle some deep emotion welling up inside. His voice wavered. "Will you tell me about that night? The night he was betrayed?"

John paused thoughtfully, repositioned his legs on the floor and took a breath. "Well, you know it was the first night of Passover. [60] Thirty-two years ago today, as a matter of fact. We'd been in the city for a few days already, and Jesus sent me—and Peter, I recall—to this large house near Herod's palace, with an opulent room upstairs. He told us to arrange the room just so, and make everything ready for his last Seder. That's how he said it—'my last Seder'. He spoke of everything with such finality during that week, and at the time all we

---

[59] See "11. Tasting the Afikoman" on page 106.

[60] See Key Passover Scriptures: "From the Gospels" on page 135.

could do was ignore it. It didn't make sense until later.

"But I remember that room so clearly. It was resplendent—the plates, the tablecloths, the furnishings. Good enough for royalty. Superior even to the homes of the Pharisees who invited us in. There was just one problem—no table servants.

"We all arrived before Jesus that evening, and started to bicker about who should serve. The last one appointed? That was Judas, but he was too important. The youngest? That was me, but I was part of Jesus' inner circle, so it didn't seem fair. (To think of how wicked I was.)

"At the height of our debate Jesus came in, carrying the lamb he had selected from the marketplace, and had taken to the Temple to be sacrificed. He had spent hours selecting it, just like you say your father used to do, but this one had a freckle on its ear. [61] We all saw it. We had the money, why didn't he choose a perfect one? But things were about to get much stranger than that.

"Peter pointed out that there was no table servant, loud enough for our host to hear. But Jesus made no expression. He just nodded, handed the lamb to the cook, and started taking off his robe. He laid it aside neatly, wrapped a towel around his waist, and *became the servant.* Jesus himself—he collected our robes, washed our feet, filled our plates; he did everything. We were dumbstruck.

"When he finally relaxed to eat with us, he reclined next to me, where I could lean my head on his chest. I was hot with shame—he had witnessed me defending my right *not* to serve, just moments before serving me. I wanted to hate myself, but he didn't let me. It was just—it was pure grace." John paused, tilted his head and smiled faintly to himself.

---

[61] See "The Imperfect Lamb" on page 84.

"Apart from that, it was a normal Seder. We drank the First Cup, and the Second Cup. We ate the parsley and the *maror,* and the lamb. It was all like usual—until we came to the breaking of the *matzah.* He said the blessing as always, but as he broke it, he added that line. 'This is my body, given for you.' We all just looked at each other. We were completely lost. But we ate anyway—and we *remembered,* like he told us to.

"Then Jesus picked up the Third Cup, and after the blessing said, 'This is my blood of the new covenant, which is poured out for many for the forgiveness of sins.' He'd talked before about having to die, but to be honest we just couldn't hear it. Even in the moment, in that upper room, we were in denial. Jesus was the Messiah! The Messiah doesn't just die. Naturally, a messiah may die *while* setting his people free, or afterwards, but not *before.* How small our faith was. We didn't see, because we didn't want to.

"But again, we drank anyway. He could tell we were confused—that we weren't ready for him to be taken from us. He knew our hearts; he told us we would all abandon him. And Peter—the chief disciple—would deny even knowing him.

"By that point we were speechless. Everything he'd said and done since we entered that room seemed to tell us that he was giving up. That we were through. Our faith would fail, Jesus would be captured and killed, his followers would disperse, and everything we'd sacrificed and believed in for three years would be scattered to the wind. And just days prior he'd been greeted with songs and cheers, riding into the Holy City like a conquering king. Most of us knew better than to contradict our Master, but we just couldn't process anything he was saying."

"At least you'd followed him." James inserted. "He had to rise from the dead before I would believe. All of us—brothers, sisters, Mother

51

even, at first—we knew he was a prophet, but didn't want to see him *rejected* like a prophet. So what did we do? We rejected him.

"We thought we were doing it out of love. But I suppose it was the wrong kind of love. [62] We loved him in a way that made us want to keep him, and not lose him to his calling. Not lose him to the world. We wouldn't give him up."

John took a deep breath and exhaled slowly. "'Whoever does the will of my Father in heaven is my brother and sister and mother.' How hard was that to hear?"

"It was impossible. Our family never recovered, until we understood. I suppose it's why Mother couldn't tell the birth story until she was in Ephesus with you. She had been the chosen vessel to bring the Messiah into the world, to raise him to adulthood. But as it turned out, even though he was her son, he wasn't really *hers*. He was our brother, but he wasn't really *ours*. He belongs to everyone. But we had to learn it the hard way. The slow way. And I was the slowest of them all."

"To be fair, it's our brother Paul who was the slowest." [63] John winked, and James snickered.

"Paul can have that prize if he wants it. But it only took Jesus a few words—and a blinding light—to get through to Paul. It took him hours to win me over. That Sunday morning, on a hillside, just the risen Jesus and me."

"He spent *hours* with you?" John asked.

"Yes." James stared silently at the wall.

"Well? At least tell me what you talked about!"

"Mother, mostly."

"Oh."

---

[62] See "The Wrong Kind of Love" on page 85.
[63] 1 Corinthians 15:9

"On the Cross—when Jesus said 'behold, your mother'—I assumed it was because you were a disciple, and none of us brothers were." [64]

"That's what I thought, too."

"But the fact is, I did become a disciple, only three days later. And when I did, Jesus told me that I was being called to "bless Jerusalem." But mother, she was being called away. Far from Judea."

John listened with his mouth agape. "So that explains—" he stammered.

"Yes. Mother knew it too," James continued. "Which is why she so readily left my house, and why she eventually boarded that ship to Ephesus with you. She knew the reason behind it, too—that the temptation of the Believers in the Land to idolize her was simply too great. She had to go away, but I had to stay here. So Jesus gave her to you."

"You say she knew the reason, but it took her a long time to accept. She thought she was being banished."

"So I gather."

"But James—all these years!"

"I know, John. I should have written to you a thousand times, to apologize, to collaborate, to broker a friendship. But my covetous nature always held me back. Sure, I understood the call. But you had something precious to me that I could never have, and I couldn't accept it. I suppose Mother and I have that in common. We have trouble letting go."

John held his peace, then responded quietly. "All is well." He lifted the silver cup again, and said the blessing over the wine. Then he added, "This is my blood of the new covenant, which is poured out for many for the forgiveness of sins." John drank, and handed the cup to

---

[64] See "Behold, Your Mother" on page 86.

James. [65]

"Worthy is the Lamb who was slain. Let us spread his blood on the doorposts of our hearts, and be saved," James recited while holding the cup. Then he drank.

"May you be blessed by ADONAI, who made heaven and earth!" John quoted the Psalm, waiting for James to reply. [66]

"The stone the builders rejected has become the cornerstone. This is the day ADONAI has made; let us rejoice and be glad in it!"

While they sang together, James recalled his Passovers as a boy in Jerusalem. John recalled Jesus leading the disciples in song on their way to the Garden. "ADONAI is my strength and my song; he has become my salvation! Give thanks to ADONAI for he is good; his love endures forever!" [67]

Sunlight was now breaking through a crack near the top of the wall, filling up the corridor outside the cell. Daylight had come. John, sensing the urgency of the moment, proceeded to the fourth and final cup. [68]

"Blessed are you, ADONAI our God, King of the Universe, who creates the fruit of the vine." John filled the cup from the wineskin, watching over his shoulder for the prison guard. He closed his eyes, and with both hands, lifted the vessel to heaven in a moment of thankfulness. The Fourth Cup. The Cup of Rejoicing.

Just then a heavy clatter jolted them out of their reverie, knocking the cup from John's hand onto the floor. A pool of red spread quickly across the ground, away from the source of the disruption. It was the guard. He had thrown the gate open, and was now towering over the

---

[65] See "12. Drinking the Cup of Redemption" on page 107.
[66] See "13. Singing the Songs of Praise (Hallel)" on page 108.
[67] Psalm 118
[68] See "14. Drinking the Cup of Joy" on page 109.

two worshipers.

"Wine?" He picked up the cup and sniffed, then threw it to the ground again. "Who is to blame for this?"

John shifted his posture to stand, but James pressed his shoulder down to prop himself up instead. "I am. I was hiding it."

"Well!" The guard snorted. "I hope you've had your fill. After all, there will be no hangover to worry about." He laughed with his throat, without cracking a smile. "Your time has come. Will you walk or be dragged?"

"I will walk," James said reverently. He bent down and retrieved the cup, brushing the dirt from its rim. "Well John, we'll have to drink the Fourth Cup together in the Kingdom, won't we?"

James handed the cup to John, who received it reluctantly. "It's my fault you didn't have it sooner," John lamented. "Shall I take it to one of your surviving brothers?"

The guard gripped James by the arm and began to tug. But before he could be moved, James answered. "John—you are my brother." And he was yanked out the door.

John followed him, taking the cup but leaving the Seder elements behind. He was double-stepping to match the pace of the guard, who was evidently not convinced of James' intent to walk. Through a maze of corridors and up a ragged staircase, they emerged into a blinding sunrise amidst a small crowd of gawkers assembled at the north Temple gate. John glanced behind him, where the Antonia Fortress was bathed in morning sunlight, with rain clouds gathering above and behind.

The guard hustled James around a corner and between two sentries. John was just three paces behind, hurrying to share a final moment with his friend. But the two sentries quickly lodged themselves in the space behind James, bringing John to a halt.

"James!" he shouted. To his surprise, James reappeared, his face between the soldiers' faces.

"Bury me in the Arimathean's tomb. [69] Like Jesus." James' countenance was clear, and all the strain had disappeared from his cheeks. John blinked hard and looked deeply into the eyes of his brother. He was already home.

"I will— I will see to it."

"I know his tomb will not raise me to new life, like my Savior, but I—" and he was gone again.

John stretched himself upward and declared through the thickening crowd, "You will be raised, James." [70] He said it once, then twice, shouting to reach his friend's ears as he moved ever closer to his fate. "You will be raised!" And then quietly to himself, as the prisoner disappeared from his sight, "We all will."

---

[69] See "Joseph of Arimathea" on page 86.
[70] 1 Corinthians 15:52

PART III

John fought the morbid curiosity of the crowd, struggling to get a last glimpse of James. And then he saw him, not being hustled by Roman thugs, but standing in front of—no, conversing with—three Jewish officials in full regalia.

He now wrestled even more fervently with the gathering, excusing himself and pushing past man, woman and child alike to gain an ear to their exchange. He could see it now—on the left was a prominent priest named Joshua ben Gamla, and on the right was the Pharisee Shimon ben Gamaliel, head of the Sanhedrin.[71] And in the center was the high priest himself: Ananus ben Ananus! A veritable triumvirate of Israel—representing both Sadducees and Pharisees.

Shimon the Pharisee spoke first. "Your reputation is like the finest silver, my dear James," he affirmed.[72] "You are known for being just—fair to all alike, and prejudicial to none. You consider the poor and the rich as one man, like we Pharisees do (as the Torah gives us strength.) So by no means should we desire that your life be dismissed in this senseless manner. Please—" He turned to the high priest for a quick exchange of whispers. James maintained his tranquil expression as he waited for the pleasantries to finish. The priest on the left spoke up.

"Please, my dear James. Spare yourself and cooperate with us. As you know, the people are gathered at the Temple for Passover, and they look to us for teaching. But so many are now entertaining

---

[71] Shimon was the leader of the Sanhedrin from AD 52 to 70. His father Gamaliel, who preceded him as leader, is famous as the teacher of the Apostle Paul, and for opposing the oppression of the Apostles in Acts 5:33-39. There is no clear evidence as to whether he decided to follow Jesus himself.

[72] See "Martyrdom of James" on page 87.

dangerous notions about this Jesus of Nazareth—your late brother, no? Yes of course."

"What would you desire of your servant?" James interjected, in full sincerity.

"We would take you to the top of the Temple wall, to address the people—your greatest audience yet. Honor your late brother, my dear James. Honor his memory by dispelling these rumors of messiahship—of kingship. Why let his good name be spoiled by such blasphemy?"

James remained silent—at once a picture of submission and stubbornness. The priest on the left started simmering with impatience, and lost his composure all at once. "Rebuke the people!" he demanded. "Tell them to abandon these erroneous opinions of the Nazarene. Set their feet aright on the path of truth."

"He will not do this!" Shimon whispered loudly to the high priest in the center. "His faith is in error, but he is a righteous man, and steadfast. If he is speaking against the Name, his message will die its own death. But if we send such a man to die, his blood will be on our heads."

Joshua the priest tried to object, but the high priest Ananus lifted his hand, requesting silence. Just then, a new face emerged from behind the three. A tall, white-bearded man leaned forward and whispered into the ear of the Ananus, who listened, then nodded.

"Save your own life, James, and thousands more as well." Ananus and James stared deeply at one another for an agonizing moment. "Address the people now. What say you?" he insisted. James turned and glanced in John's direction, then turned back to Ananus, closed his eyes and drew a long, deep breath.

"I will go. I will persuade the people to abandon their erroneous opinions of the Nazarene."

John gasped. He stood frozen as the priests walked off in the direction of the Temple, and the guards pulled James behind them. The calm expression never left James' face, but John could see his eyes darting as he followed the priests along the incline and through the Temple's northern gate. The holiday throng parted for the James' procession like the waters before Moses. But they did not part for John, as he trotted up the hill, trying not to lose sight of his friend.

John entered the Outer Court and was immediately assaulted by the raucous noise of the Passover crowd. Vendors from every nation on earth, hustling in every direction and shouting every known language, selling their ceremonial merchandise to travelers and natives alike. There was no way to locate James in the crowd, until John glanced up and spotted him at the corner of the southern wall, still preceded by the three officials, and manhandled by the guards.

They walked until they reached the highest point of the wall. The high priest halted the party, and turned James to face the Kidron Valley to the east, a fifteen-story drop from their place at the top of the Temple. After considering the height for a moment, they made their way across the thickness of the wall to stand on the inside edge overlooking the crowd, which gradually turned and began to notice the proceedings above.

The priests waited patiently, as all commerce and conversation ground to a halt. *Here is an embattled prisoner,* the crowd realized, *about to speak to the gathering at sword-point.* Some recognized him as a follower of Jesus. *Isn't this his brother? And the head of the Nazarene sect in Jerusalem? This should be worth hearing.*

"I am James," he muttered, clearing his throat noisily. The guard jabbed at his back, and he could feel the skin break. "I am James!" he shouted for the whole assembly to hear. "Brother of Jesus, the Nazarene!" John snaked carefully through the crowd, closer to his friend, until he was directly underneath, squeezed into a gaggle of scribes and Pharisees. He listened and prayed with the whole of his being as James' voice gathered strength.

"You know this name! Many have undertaken to spread falsehoods about him throughout Judea, Samaria and the ends of the earth. I am here to dispel these falsehoods." He paused to scan the assembly, allowing his introduction to sink in.

"Some claim that Jesus was born in the line of David, to a virgin, our mother Mary." The crowd grumbled, and James continued, growing louder with each sentence. "Some claim that he healed the blind and the lepers, and raised our Lazarus from death, who is with us today. Some claim that he walked upon waters, and calmed a raging tempest on the Galilee. Some claim that he divided a small boy's meal to feed a vast gathering of followers."

Ananus was fidgeting. He was starting to doubt his decision, but James pressed on. "You all know that this Jesus was crucified at Golgotha." He pointed across the Temple compound toward the western gate of the city, where the site of the crucifixion and the famous tomb were now contained inside the expanded city wall. "Some of you stood witness. Some of you know that he was laid in the tomb of Joseph the Arimathean. And you all know that, three days later, his body was gone."

So far he's kept it factual, John thought to himself. *No one denies the empty tomb. But where is he taking this?*

"Some believe his body was stolen by his followers. Others believe he was raised from the dead. The Baptizer called him the Passover Lamb, the final sacrifice. He and many others were punished for teaching that he was the Son of David, the Son of Man, the Son of God!"

The high priest was angry. The crowd was shouting. The guard

61

removed his sword from the prisoner's back and pressed it to his neck. James held up his hands. "Please! Please! My brothers! Listen to me. This Jesus has divided us. He has not brought peace to the Land—as we believed the Messiah should—but a sword! See for yourself." The roar quieted to a murmur.

"This dispute can be settled, and our people reunited, with one simple question: Where is Jesus now?" The people nodded. "Was his body laid in another tomb? Was it burned and scattered to the four winds? None of these, I tell you. He is not laid prostrate in a tomb in Jerusalem or contained in an ossuary in Galilee. I tell you this instead: Jesus is seated in the heavens at the right hand of ADONAI—our Passover Lamb forever!"

Ananus gnashed his teeth but remained still. Suddenly, I saw the white bearded man standing atop the wall off to the right of John. Then half a dozen figures in black robes emerged from where the man was standing, running toward James along the top of the wall. Leaders of the Pharisees!

The one in the lead gestured aggressively to the guards, who wrenched James away from his audience. But he continued anyway, speaking louder and faster. "I see him descending through the clouds! Clothed in righteousness to take away our sin. To save us—not from the Romans, but from ourselves!" And in a moment, James disappeared over the edge.

John rushed toward the gate below, but so did everyone else. He slithered his way through as best he could, but found himself locked into a frenzied mob, chanting rhythmically, "Stone him! Stone him! Stone him!"

John's knees buckled in shock, but he didn't fall. Instead he was carried along by the crowd, out the gate and onto the staircase overlooking the valley. Apart from the crush of humanity on his left and right, behind and before, he couldn't see a thing.

He was alone.

––––––––––––––––––––

Half an hour later, the crowd was gone. Two sentries were all who remained, tasked with wrapping the body to prepare it for burial there on the valley floor. As they worked, John approached the site of the deed. [73] The sentries paused and looked up. James' body was already tightly shrouded, and the cloth at the back of his head was seeping blood.

"Do not bury him here in the valley, where Absalom lies." John tried to remain calm as he made his appeal. His ears were ringing so badly, he worried that he might be shouting. "Here, take him to the tomb of Joseph the Arimathean, and ask for Priscilla. I will join you there."

He plugged a denarius into the hand of each, and watched as the younger one ran to a guard room beneath the Temple to summon two more sentries and a stretcher. They wrapped the body one more time, then hustled it up the stairs, stopping briefly to pay homage to a richly robed man on the landing. John looked and saw it was Shimon ben Gamaliel, standing still at a distance from James' body—his head bowed, and his tunic ripped.

The Passover throng was still in full force overhead, but the valley around him was empty. Soon enough John would follow the sentries to the tomb to commit his friend's body to burial. But for the moment he felt like his head was trapped inside a water jug. He removed his shoes, collapsed to his knees, and wept.

––––––––––––––––

[73] See "John's Response" on page 89.

After some time, John raised himself up, dried his face, grabbed his tunic at the neck with both hands, and ripped it down the middle. Top to bottom. [74]

The rain began to fall, and he heard the crowds rushing to take cover in the Temple porticoes. As the drops worked their way into his clothes and hair, John felt his heart being steadied by the Spirit. The ringing sound subsided as the physical shock began to wane. Gradually a new sound came to his ears from the Temple gates above. At first it was muddled, but as he tuned his hearing to it, the words became clear.

"Hosanna to the Son of David! Save us, Son of David! Hosanna to the Son of David! Save us, Son of David!" Fresh tears emerged on John's face and mingled with the rain. He heard the chant repeated over and over, growing to a roar that echoed in the valley and shook the hills.

John stood up and wrapped his robe around his shredded tunic, hugging his chest and listening with his entire body. The words of Isaiah came bubbling up from his soul, and flowed like a fountain from his lips, "In my Temple and within my walls, I will give them a name better than sons and daughters. I will give them an everlasting name that will not be cut off." [75]

An everlasting name. The name of Jesus.

Suddenly, the blast of a shofar [76] ripped through the storm and split the sky. The crowd was silenced, and John fell to his knees again. It was the third hour, and the priests on the wall were signaling the first Passover sacrifice. Since the day his Messiah was crucified, John could no longer hear the Temple shofar without being transported

---

[74] Matthew 27:51
[75] Isaiah 56:5
[76] Ram's horn, or trumpet

back to Golgotha.

As the sound crescendoed in his skull, his vision was consumed with the grisly sight of the once-and-forever Passover Lamb, stretched and suffering like a filthy traitor. All his followers had scattered, and John himself was barely hanging on. One wrong move and he'd be the next victim hoisted on a cross.

I don't want to die, he fretted, *but how can I live without Jesus?* Still, he kept his distance. John felt his stomach wrench, as his body flooded with shame all over again.

The shofar pealed a second time, and John shook his head. He looked up to see the walls of the city above him—now rattling and quaking violently. The shouts of the people and the blast of the shofar continued to erupt, like Jericho from the inside out.

Then, to John's horror the capstone at the peak of the Temple broke free from its perch and started to tumble. Other stones came with it, and he watched helplessly as the ancient wall started to collapse all around him. He feared for his life, but he couldn't budge. Finally a massive stone hurtled toward him from above, and *thud—* His vision went dark.

In an instant John came back to himself, and the shofar sounded a third and final time, long and loud. The wall was still there. "Forgive them," he panted. "They didn't know what they were doing."

At length, John's heart was calm again. He returned to his feet, and began moving back and forth to examine the scene of the murder. He saw stones littered about—some smooth, some sharp. He picked up a pointed one that looked small enough for a child to throw, and contemplated its handler.

The chants resumed, quietly at first, then louder. John looked up at the Temple, then down at the sand beneath his feet. He kneeled reverently and whispered a blessing. Then he touched the tip of the rock to the ground and started drawing in the sand.

Slowly he traced out one letter and then another—one word and then another, writing a prayer that only he would ever read.

Epilogue

Saturday Evening, the 16th of Nisan

"Thirty-two years ago I, John son of Zebedee, found myself at this very tomb. [77] This is where everything changed. This place of death became, for me and for all of us, a place of restoration, where life could begin. Like the body of our Messiah, we entered the darkness as dead men and emerged into the light, as those reborn.

"Now this tomb has become a place of darkness again to me. We tear our robes for our brother James, yet we do not grieve as though we are hopeless. Because the Messiah lives, our hope is not in vain."

The anguish was etched into John's face as he spoke. Whatever miracle he imagined—we all imagined—had not come to pass. James was dead. Did we doubt? Did we lack faith? Have we become so accustomed to seeing our leaders martyred that we've stopped believing for their rescue?

I looked around at my brothers and sisters, beating their chests, rending their garments, and asked God if we'd resigned ourselves to this from the day James was arrested.

---

[77] See "James' Tomb" on page 92.

JAMES *of* NAZARETH
SON *of* JOSEPH
BROTHER *of* JESUS

The hillside facing the tomb was soon choked with mourners.
People were flooding the valley, even beyond sight of the tomb, just to
be near him. Passover festivities continued on the other side of the
city, and I wondered to myself if the crowd over there was noticeably
smaller as a result.

Next to John was Simon, the oldest surviving son of Joseph and
Mary. John commissioned him to take up his brother's mantle, and
the leadership of the community of Believers at Jerusalem. He was not
weeping, but he stood still clenching and unclenching his jaw,
determining to stay strong for the journey ahead. On my left (and
Simon's right) was Jude, and on my right were James' sisters. All of
his siblings were in one place, except for Joses who left for Rome the
day before James was incarcerated. Poor Joses—he won't learn of his
brother's death for another week.

After John's words of committal, Nicolas the Deacon of Jerusalem
stepped up to lift a prayer to heaven in memory of his dear friend
James. It reminded me of Moses on the mountain overlooking the
promised land—or maybe Solomon dedicating the Temple. Wherever
his words had come from, they were simply stunning. The crowd
agreed. His prayer moved us into to a collective wail and a burst of
applause, after which we proceeded to mourn freely for the better part
of an hour. Fervent and passionate prayers arose in more languages
than I could count—tongues of men and angels.

As the prayers were waning Jude found me. I've always liked Jude because he never wasted a single moment, or a single word. And he tried to never miss an opportunity to be about his Brother's work. While others were weeping, his eyes remained dark and dense. After getting my attention, he handed me a little scroll. I opened it discreetly, and saw a single page of Hebrew text. I looked up again, and Jude nodded gravely. *You know what to do,* he seemed to say.[78]

I rolled up the scroll and put it in my cloak, right next to the one from James. There was still so much we didn't know, so much ahead that was dark to us. But there was work enough to translate the light we did know—the beauty we had already seen.

At length, John resumed his standing position and turned to face the multitude. He opened his mouth and spoke, and as he faced the grieving multitude his voice seemed to reach every corner of the throng.

"May this earthen vessel now be committed to the dust from whence it came, and one year from now [79] be placed in a suitable ossuary [80] for burial in the company of Joseph of Nazareth and his fathers. Likewise may ADONAI bless the name of Joseph the Arimathean, who has again offered this tomb for a higher purpose.

"*Baruch atah ADONAI Eloheinu Melech haOlam, dayan haEmet.*" Blessed are you ADONAI our God, King of the Universe. The True Judge."

Amen. Come quickly, Jesus. I added under my breath. *Come quickly.*

---

[78] Priscilla is referring to the Epistle of Jude
[79] See "Proclaiming "Next Year in Jerusalem"" on page 110.
[80] A box which serves as the final resting place of human remains.

THE TEACHING

Commentary on the Story

Note: This section is intended as a reference. The notes herein may be read sequentially, or simply referred to as needed. Characterizations and plot points described in this section are believed by the authors to be feasible and realistic. However, they are not specifically supported by historical evidence, unless otherwise indicated.

Prologue

The Zealots (p. 13)

Walking just ahead of Priscilla, John and company on the approach to Jerusalem is a band of Zealots, with violent intentions. Zealots were a revolutionary sect of the Jewish people, who believed that the only way to restore the Kingdom to Israel, was to muster a military uprising against the forces of Rome. One of Jesus' twelve disciples, Simon the Zealot, came from this sect—though he likely modified his views under the influence of his rabbi Jesus.

Translation (p. 17)

Priscilla's character is developed in the Passover Trilogy as a religious teacher and classically trained scribe. Since she is presented in Scripture as a resident of Ephesus, like John the Apostle, the story supposes that she assists John with translating and editing his work— namely, the canonical First Epistle of John. In turn, the quality of her work on this document may have commended her to other Apostles, such as James and Jude.

Some scholarly objections to James' authorship of his namesake epistle exist, due to his presumably limited grasp of the Greek language. (History assumes that he never traveled widely, like many of his contemporaries, and remained firmly rooted in his Hebrew and Aramaic context.) However, if the letter was written in Hebrew and translated into Greek for distribution by an associate like Priscilla, such authorship objections disappear.

Part I

James' Late Mother (p. 24)

This scene features a tense conversation between James and John about the handling of the remains of Mary, the mother of James and Jesus.

For the sake of the narrative, the authors presume that James and John had a rocky relationship during their respective ministries. Although this presumption is made for the purpose of literary intrigue, it is not unrealistic. The fact that Jesus, on the cross, committed his mother Mary's care to the young disciple John (instead of to his own brother and next-of-kin James) may have generated some friction between the two. When John subsequently departed for his mission field in Ephesus, and presumably took Mary with him, the tension may have been heightened further still.

James is one of the most revered fathers of the historical Christian Church. However, his reluctance to believe in Jesus prior to the resurrection may hint at some cynical aspect in his character, which is used to propel the drama in the story. Although at this stage in his life, James has grown tremendously in the Spirit, and made historic achievements for the foundation of the Church, the authors suppose that he may still have one lingering flaw: his bitterness toward John. It is James' need to resolve this attitude, before he dies, that forms the emotional and relational foundation of the story.

Thus, when John alone arrives on the last night of James' life, James is not thrilled. He challenges John regarding the burial of Mary, assuming that he has forgotten about her since her death, and left her buried forever in a foreign land. Instead, he is mildly surprised to learn that John has brought Mary's bones with him, to bury them permanently in Jerusalem. Although it is presumed in the story that this is done discreetly, church history supports Jerusalem as the final resting place of Mary. John of Damascus writes in the 8th century that Empress Pulcheria requested that the Bishop of Jerusalem transport her bones to Constantinople in AD 458. It is unclear whether this request was granted.

James' Cup (p. 25)

The cup John offers James is the one which would have passed to Jesus upon his father's death, and then to John as the honorary heir named by Jesus on the cross.

Although Jesus likely carried almost nothing of value during his ministry, it is reasonable to assume that if he carried one precious item, it might have been the "family cup". And despite the apparent poverty of his family of origin, an ornate but modest silver goblet may have been retained as a precious heirloom.

As the most likely cup to be used at the Last Supper, this artifact is traditionally referred to as the Holy Grail. If John did indeed acquire it, as the story supposes, no one knows quite what he did with it.

Seder Elements (p. 26)

As is stated in the Introduction, the Seder depicted in this story is not intended to be historically accurate to first-century practice. Since the purpose of this book is, in part, to educate the reader about current Passover traditions, certain modern practices have been superimposed onto this first-century setting.

Washing of the Feet (p. 28)

Although there is no evidence that the apostles washed feet during Seder celebrations, it is not unreasonable to suppose that this might have become normative, based on the example of Jesus at the Last Supper.

It is interesting to note that, in some church traditions, a foot-washing ritual is observed during the Maundy Thursday service, which commemorates the Last Supper.

Mikveh (p. 28)

A *mikveh* is a ritual immersion basin. The Jewish practice of cleansing in a *mikveh* served as a fore-runner of the Christian sacrament of baptism. This is the ritual that was behind the scene Christians refer to as the "baptism" of Jesus. Although it was often associated with repentance for sin, it also served the purpose of ritual cleansing, prior to the celebration of certain holidays, or entrance to the Temple. First-century Christians may have continued to observe this as a regular practice, wholly apart from the sacrament of baptism, which only occurs once in a person's life.

Pilgrimage Festivals (p. 30)

James recalls memories of having journeyed to Jerusalem twice a year with his family, once for Passover and once for Sukkot (the Feast of Tabernacles). Whenever possible, families traveling to the city for Passover would stay an additional seven weeks in order to be present for Shavuot (the Feast of Weeks, or Pentecost) as well. Because of the tradition of traveling to Jerusalem for Passover, Shavuot and Sukkot, these three holidays are referred to as the "Pilgrimage Festivals".

These were very special times to be found worshiping in the Temple, and celebrating with fellow Jews in obedience to the Torah. These three also hold vital significance for the redemptive plan of God through Jesus, which forms the central theme of the Passover Trilogy.

Samaria (p. 30)

Samaria was the territory between Galilee in the north and Judea in the south. Here the Samaritans lived at odds with the Jews in both Galilee and Judea.

Galileans traveling to Jerusalem had three routes to choose from: (1) through the hill country of Samaria, (2) along the western bank of the Jordan River, which serves as a boundary for Samaria, or (3) the King's Highway, which followed the eastern bank of the Jordan, outside of Samaritan territory.

Option 1 was highly unfavorable to Jewish people, due to their historic antipathy toward Samaritans. (This is why it's so notable that Jesus and his disciples used this route in the story of the Samaritan woman at the well, in John chapter four.) Option 3 avoids the Samaritans altogether, but it may have been expensive, due to the need to hire a ferry to cross the Jordan River twice.

Thus, travelers of modest means would have used option 2, traveling uncomfortably through Samaritan territory, albeit along the edge.

Songs of Ascent (p. 31)

The fifteen Songs of Ascent come from Psalms 120-134. These brief Psalms were sung in the Temple services, and by travelers as they ascended the road leading to Jerusalem. Following are a few of the best-known passages.

121:1-2 "I will lift up my eyes to the mountains— from where does my help come? My help comes from ADONAI, Maker of heaven and earth."

122:6 "Pray for the peace of Jerusalem—May those who love you be at peace!"

124:2-3 "Had ADONAI not been on our side, when men rose up against us, then they would have swallowed us alive, when their wrath burned against us."

125:2 "As the mountains are around Jerusalem, so ADONAI is all around His people, both now and forever."

126:5-6 "Those who sow in tears will reap with a song of joy. Whoever keeps going out weeping, carrying his bag of seed, will surely come back with a song of joy, carrying his sheaves."

127:1 "Unless ADONAI builds the house, the builders labor in vain. Unless ADONAI watches over the city, the watchman stands guard in vain."

130:3-4 "If You, ADONAI, kept a record of iniquities—my Lord, who could stand? For with You there is forgiveness, so You may be revered."

133:1 "Behold, how good and how pleasant it is for brothers to dwell together in unity!"

134:1-3 "Behold, bless ADONAI, all servants of ADONAI, who stand by night in the House of ADONAI. Lift up your hands to the Sanctuary and bless ADONAI. May ADONAI bless you out of Zion—Maker of heaven and earth."

Jesus at Twelve (p. 33)

The second chapter of Luke describes Jesus in the Temple at age twelve, baffling the religious leaders with his questions. Although Bar Mitzvah traditions would not begin for hundreds of years, this was roughly the age that Jewish boys were trusted with adult responsibilities in the Temple and Synagogue. Thus, this is also the age that Jesus' father may have begun trusting him with the selection of the Passover lamb.

John the Baptizer (p. 33)

More commonly known as John the Baptist, he is referred to as the Baptizer in this story, to avoid confusion with modern-day Baptist Christians. Messianic Jews often call him John the Immerser.

Some might argue fairly from Scripture that John never met Jesus before his baptism. This story presumes however, that as cousins, a friendship between them would be highly plausible.

Although John is revered as a saint by Christians, James' anecdotes here are a good reminder that he would not have been known for "saintly" behavior in his own day. John strongly challenged the prevailing religious attitude of his day and time, calling Israel to a place of repentance. He behaved in ways that would have been viewed as erratic, such as living in the wilderness, eating locusts and honey and wearing clothes made of camel skin.

Some have concluded that John the Baptizer, as the son of a Temple priest, was actually the true high priest appointed by God, and that the official high priest was a counterfeit, along with the rest of the secularized and corrupted Temple system. As the true high priest, it would have been well within John's authority to name Jesus as the "Lamb of God which takes away the sin of the world" (An obvious Passover reference - John 1:29) and to baptize him as the coming high priest for all time, in the order of Melchizedek. (Psalm 110, Hebrews chapters 5–7)

In turn, Jesus confirmed John's role as the "second Elijah" (Matthew 11:14) which explains two tongue-in-cheek references in this story: (1) his mother going into labor during a Seder, at the moment when the imaginary Elijah is expected to arrive, and (2) his adolescent prank dressing up as Elijah to surprise everyone at the door. All playfulness aside, many scholars have concluded that John was indeed born during Passover, based on the details provided about the timing of his father's assigned shift at the Temple, and his prompt return to his wife after that shift had ended. (Luke 1:5)

Elijah (p. 34)

The prophet Elijah is the honored guest at every Seder, with a special cup and sometimes even a place setting. At one point in the Seder ritual, the door is opened to receive him, even though he is not expected to be there. There is also a song honoring Elijah which is traditionally sung at Passover Seders: "Eliyahu Ha-Navi", or "Elijah the Prophet".

Elijah's symbolic presence at the Seder is a representation of the messianic prophecy and hope embedded in the ritual. This reality is enhanced by the idea of a Passover birth for John the Baptizer (see commentary note above.)

Oral Tradition (p. 35)

Zechariah tells the story of John the Baptizer's birth exactly the same way every year. Although this is an imaginary scene, it highlights the importance and reliability of the Oral Tradition in Jewish culture. This was a highly developed skill amongst the Jewish people, enabling them to memorize huge volumes of information and transmit them orally from one generation to the next without error.

Death of Joseph (p. 35)

Many scholars have concluded that Joseph—the father of Jesus, James and others—died when Jesus was a young man. This is based largely on the failure of the Gospels to make any mention of him after Jesus was twelve, and the fact that Jesus had apparently assumed headship over his family by the time of his crucifixion. This is the responsibility he passed to John on the cross. (John 19:26)

The Red Sea (p. 38)

There is some debate among scholars regarding the Israelites' crossing of the Red Sea. While it is true that *Yam Suph* is better translated "Reed Sea", there is no direct evidence as to exactly which body of water this refers to. Some have concluded that it was a shallow marshy lake (now dry) located directly east of Goshen. On the other hand, it's worth noting that both northern branches of the Red Sea (Gulfs of Suez and Aqaba) have been referred to in Scripture as *Yam Suph*, or the Reed Sea.

Moses' destination, upon departing Egypt, was not Canaan as many imagine, but Midian. Back when he encountered the burning bush in Midian, God told him that a sign of his promise would be the people's return to worship on that very mountain. (Exodus 3:12) This is a reference to Mount Horeb, which came to be known as Sinai. The land of Midian was located east of the Gulf of Aqaba, fully outside Egyptian territory. Thus, Mount Sinai could not have been located on the (mis-named) Sinai peninsula, because that peninsula was not in Midian, but rather within the territory of Egypt.

The accurate location of Mount Sinai would be in the northwestern corner of modern-day Saudi Arabia. This is confirmed by one proposed location of the Israelites' miraculous crossing, at the Gulf of Aqaba (Red Sea) called *Nuwayba' al Muzayyinah,* which is Arabic for "Waters of Moses Opening". This spot has several features which support the Exodus story: (1) a wadi leading from the west which could have served as a road for both the Israelites, and the pursuing Egyptian army, (2) an enormous beachhead on the shoreline, where millions of people could potentially congregate, and (3) a shallow sea floor "bridge" across the gulf, which could facilitate a smooth crossing.

Additionally, archaeologists have uncovered countless chariot wheels on the sea floor, scattered along this stretch, as well as an ancient pillar on each shore, apparently erected by King Solomon to mark the location of the miracle.

Considering all this, there is a high likelihood that the Israelites did indeed cross the expanse we know today as the Red Sea. Therefore, it is appropriate to refer to the body of water either as the Reed Sea (or Sea of Reeds) because that is the most accurate translation, or as the Red Sea, because that is the name of the most historically probable location.

The latter is chosen for this story, because it supports the traditional understanding of the event, and does not distract the reader by appearing to call the historicity of the miracle account into question.

Mary (p. 41)

It is a common view that Mary, like her second son James, struggled to accept the reality of Jesus' calling during his ministry. (Matthew 12:46-50) It is presumed that she did not follow him fully until his crucifixion and resurrection. In hindsight, this would likely have caused her a great amount of guilt, and the feeling of having failed her son when he needed her. This is why the story presumes her to have been reluctant to tell her story in Ephesus. Perhaps it took her some time to feel truly forgiven of her initial lack of trust, and worthy of spreading such a powerful gospel account.

This inward struggle may have been the one Simeon prophesied to Mary in Luke 2:35, "...even for you, a sword will pierce through your soul."

Sukkot (p. 42)

Sukkot, or the Feast of Tabernacles, is one of the three Pilgrimage Festivals, and the last of the seven festivals outlined in Leviticus chapter twenty-three. During Sukkot, which lasts eight days, each observant Jewish family builds and occupies a Sukkah, or small three-sided booth with a view of the stars.

Some scholars have concluded that Jesus was born during *Sukkot*. This is based on John's use of the word Tabernacle in John 1:14, "and the Word was made flesh, and dwelt [or 'Tabernacled'] among us." It is also drawn from the timeline of John the Baptizer's birth, in the spring, being six months prior to that of Jesus. This would result in a birthdate between late September and mid-October, which may have corresponded to the festival of Sukkot.

Part II

Feeding the Multitude (p. 47)

Otherwise known as the "Feeding of the 5,000" this is one of the few miracles recorded in all four gospels. In a scene that occurs just prior to Passover, Jesus tells his disciples, "You give them something to eat," indicating that he is entrusting them with spiritual power. The synoptic gospels all affirm this by adding that Jesus handed them the pieces of broken bread and fish, to subsequently hand to the people.

Mark 6:40 adds an interesting detail in regard to the numbers of the people. The crowd on the hillside is instructed to sit down in groups of "hundreds and of fifties" which can be interpreted to mean groups of 150. If there were indeed 5,000 men, as Mark records, it is plausible that the total size of the crowd might have been roughly twice that. If the total number was close to 10,500, it may have indicated that the purpose of the grouping was to give each of the Seventy disciples one manageable group to serve.

It should be noted that this is merely a plausible theory on the part of the authors of this book. Nevertheless, it is difficult to find any other rational explanation for the synoptic gospels' inclusion of the size of the groups on the hillside.

The Imperfect Lamb (p. 50)

As mentioned before, Jesus would have celebrated Passover every year of his life, with his family. But Jesus took a different approach to the Seder in his thirty-third year. As we know, he was prepared to go to the Cross the very next day, to become the slaughtered Lamb for all of humankind, receiving the punishment for our sin and banishing the Angel of Death once and for all. The millions of perfect lambs which had been sacrificed over the years since the Exodus were now

84

officially obsolete.

Nevertheless, Jesus and his disciples still needed a lamb. They needed it to serve its symbolic role in the Passover Seder, and they also needed something to eat for dinner. But the lamb no longer needed to be perfect. The perfect and ultimate sacrifice had already arrived.

This reality was not a secret, to be uncovered by future generations. Jesus made it painfully obvious to his own disciples right there at the Seder. The Passover wine that had always symbolized the blood of the slaughtered lamb was now to represent his own blood shed at Golgotha. And the yeast-less bread would now be broken to remind them of his sinless body, nailed to the Cross. (And yet, like the lamb, no bones were broken.)

The Wrong Kind of Love (p. 52)

Jesus said, "Whoever is not against us is for us." (Mark 9:40) This sounds familiar to modern ears, but is actually the opposite of the more common sentiment, "Whoever is not for us is against us."

From the first days of Jesus' ministry till now, the temptation has existed among believers to "claim" Jesus as their own, to the exclusion of others. Mary, James and his other siblings struggled with this, as James expresses to John in the story. Believers today also must come to terms with the radical welcome that Jesus expressed in his preaching, his works, and most importantly, on the Cross. God chose the Jewish people in order to make them a blessing to the whole world, and in Jesus, this purpose comes to fruition. May we never play the role of gatekeeper, demanding that all those drawn to him must identify and assimilate with us. May we never try to keep Jesus to ourselves.

Behold, Your Mother (p. 53)

There are multiple biblical references implicit in this brief exchange between James and John. First is the statement of Jesus on the Cross, directed to his beloved disciple John, and his mother Mary: "Behold your son ... Behold your mother." (John 19:26-27) Since Mary's husband Joseph was probably deceased, and Jesus had spent the last three years in itinerant ministry, it can be presumed that Mary as a widow would have been primarily entrusted to her next-oldest son James. It would seem reasonable for Jesus to entrust her care to his disciple John, instead, since James and the brothers had persisted in their unbelief.

But then, just three days later, James becomes a disciple himself. 1 Corinthians 15:7 lists James among the first people to whom the risen Jesus appeared. Since James is believed to have finally become a disciple of Jesus at the time of his resurrection (see Acts 1:14) it is reasonable that this personal appearance may have served as a "conversion experience" for James.

Now that James was a disciple, one might expect him to then resume the care of his widowed mother. After all, what reason remains for her to go with John? But she does indeed go with him.

Although the rationale provided in this exchange is fictional, it attempts to provide a reason for Mary's continued association with John instead of her own blood relatives, even to the point of eventually relocating to Ephesus.

Joseph of Arimathea (p. 56)

All four Gospel accounts credit Joseph of Arimathea with the lending of his tomb for the burial of Jesus. As stated before, a tomb like this would have been considered a place of temporary repose, usually for one year, after which time the bones would be collected into an ossuary and buried in the ground.

Some point to Joseph as the fulfillment of the messianic prophecy in Isaiah 53:9, "His grave was given ... by a rich man in his death."

Joseph himself was a Pharisee, and a member of the Sanhedrin, or Jewish ruling council. But he differed from most of his fellow elders in his openness to the messiahship of Jesus. This subversion would have caused a great deal of friction, and likely threatened the security of his position. Some have theorized (particularly in Arthurian legend) that Joseph was given responsibility for the Holy Grail. However, there is no apparent historical credibility to this assumption.

The real significance of his character, like that of Nicodemus or Gamaliel, is in the degree of risk imposed by his act of faith, and the amount he stood to lose by following Jesus.

Part III

Martyrdom of James (p. 58)

A number of accounts exist, of varying degrees of reliability, regarding the manner of James' death. The most well-known are by the historians Josephus, Clement of Alexandria, and Hegesippus.

The last of the three is the most detailed, and appears to be an attempt to reconcile previous, otherwise contradictory accounts. Hegesippus records that James was approached by the high priest Ananus ben Ananus, who flattered him with references to his reputation as a just and fair-minded man. He assumed that a man with his character, and close family ties to Jesus, would be able to persuade the people to abandon their "erroneous opinions" of him.

The timing could not have been more perfect. It was the first morning of Passover, and an enormous crowd of people from every corner of the diaspora were gathered at the Temple. Anyone escorted by the high priest to the pinnacle of the outer wall was certain to gain the attention of the throng.

The tallest wall in the Second Temple compound was located at the southeast corner, overlooking the arid Kidron Valley. When looking up from the valley, this fifteen-story wall so impressed viewers that it came to be known as the "pinnacle" of the Temple (referenced in the temptation of Jesus, Matthew 4:5.) When facing east, the drop-off was menacing, but facing west afforded an overview of the largest section of the massive Outer Court (or Court of the Gentiles.) Thus, a speaker standing on this point on the first day of Passover may have been able to address up to one hundred thousand people!

As the story reveals, James was given just such an audience by the high priest, in hopes that he would speak against the messiahship of Jesus. However, the threat of a deadly fall had no such effect. He began his speech with an appeal to the priests' request, granting that many were spreading falsehoods about Jesus, but with the opposite meaning.

Next, James recalls the works of Jesus, which were still circulating among the people more than three decades later. He continues with a reference to the missing body, thus appealing to common ground, and stretching his argument as far as possible before showing his hand. No one denies the missing body. If it were not missing, someone would have it. But no one does.

It looks like James will pivot here, but he buys just another minute more by calming his seething audience with confidence and charisma. He reminds them that Jesus has divided them as a people, which is true. (Matthew 10:34) So he offers a plan of reconciliation: If they could all agree as to the whereabouts of Jesus, Israel could be united again.

At this moment James has a vision, recorded specifically by Hegesippus:

To the scribes' and Pharisees' dismay, James boldly testified that "Christ himself sitteth in heaven, at the right hand of the Great Power, and shall come on the clouds of heaven." The scribes and Pharisees then said to themselves, "We have not done well in procuring this testimony to Jesus. But let us go up and throw him down, that they may be afraid, and not believe him." [81]

In the story, James proclaims this vision to the crowd, along with a declaration that Jesus is the Passover Lamb forever. In essence, he is saying that everything they knew about Passover has been fulfilled. Something far better is here. The once-and-forever Lamb has arrived, making the Temple ritual obsolete.

This, of course, is all the Pharisees need to hear. They appear on the wall to commandeer the situation, and in an instant, James is pushed over the edge. According to the record, however, he is not killed by the impact. Thus, another collection of angry scribes and Pharisees picks up stones to finish the job. Although this may appear to be nothing more than an attempt by Hegesippus to reconcile disparate accounts, it's actually consistent with contemporary practice. Often a prisoner was executed by being thrown off a cliff, head first, and stoned at the bottom if not killed by the fall.

John's Response (p. 63)

John is now racked with grief, tearing his robe beyond repair, and collapsing to mourn the loss of his spiritual brother. However, he soon discovers that the murderous scribes and Pharisees he'd been surrounded with were not representative of the entire gathering. As

---

[81] Eusebius' Ecclesiastical History, vol. II, ch. 23

Hegesippus records, the Temple crowd-at-large responds to James' address by crying out again and again, "Hosanna to the Son of David!" [82]

While the crowd is still chanting, the third hour of the day (9 A.M.) arrives, which is the time for the first Passover sacrifice. [83] This moment is marked by three shofar blasts, traditionally sounded from the same point of the Temple where James made his final stand. John observes all this, and is overwhelmed by the Spirit of God, entering into a pair of back-to-back visions.

With the first shofar, John receives a vision from the past. He is vividly reminded of the sight he encountered on the Cross, watching his beloved Messiah suffer and die like an animal (namely, a lamb.) John is wrenched anew with the feelings of guilt he experienced by not supporting Jesus in his suffering.

With the second shofar, he is terrified to witness the Temple wall giving way to the shouts of the people and the blasts of the ram's horn. The stones begin tumbling all around him, appearing to threaten his life. This is a vision of near-future events, which will be featured in the upcoming third book of the Passover Trilogy.

The third shofar brings him back to the present. When the visions are over, John hears the chanting resume, giving him the strength to keep his promise to James, and see to the proper treatment of his remains. But first, he takes a queue from Jesus (John 8:6-8) and records his thoughts in the sand. Unfortunately, the words do not last long enough to be read by anyone. The rain washes them away.

---

[82] Matthew 21:9 (also see "Psalm 118:21-26" on page 109.)

[83] Originally, the Passover sacrifice occurred only at the ninth hour (3 P.M.) but eventually so many sacrifices were needed that they came to be performed twice a day, every day. Thus, the first sacrifice to be performed during Passover would take place at the third hour, on the first morning of the festival.

Like John's second vision in the story, some historians believe the martyrdom of James really did mark the beginning of the end for the Second Temple, and for the city of Jerusalem as he knew it. His unjust execution set political wheels in motion which purportedly led to the Roman siege on the city, and ultimately its downfall.

Whether this connection is justified or not, James' execution belongs to a host of events which reveal the heart of the city's leaders in those final days, echoing the words of Jesus in Matthew 23:37, "O Jerusalem, Jerusalem who kills the prophets and stones those sent to her! How often I longed to gather your children together, as a hen gathers her chicks under her wings, but you were not willing! Look, your house is left to you desolate! For I tell you, you will never see Me again until you say, blessed is He who comes in the name of the Lord!" [84]

History suggests that the Passover gathering that year was swayed by James' message, but apparently the powers-that-be were unconvinced.

In modern times we celebrate Passover as a joyful celebration of God's master story of redemption. We enter in to the suffering and uncertainty of the past, and we pray like Jesus did for the soon-coming redemption of Israel and Jerusalem. We owe our very salvation to the faithfulness of the Jewish people throughout history, and now we long to pay this hope in Messiah forward, to the place, and the people, in which it was founded.

---

[84] Here Jesus quotes from the *Hallel,* Psalm 118:26. (See "13. Singing the Songs of Praise *(Hallel)*", p. 108)

Epilogue

James' Tomb (p. 67)

It was standard practice in this place and time for a body to lie in a tomb like that of Joseph of Arimathea for a period of one year, then be transferred to a small ossuary, or bone box, for permanent burial.

Although John is in a state of deep mourning for his friend in this scene, he takes the opportunity to reference the transformative power of the resurrection of Jesus, which had taken place on that very site some thirty-two years prior. He finishes his address with a common Jewish blessing offered in moments of grief.

Passover

Passover is the first of seven festivals outlined by ADONAI according in Leviticus 23:4-8. According to verse four, "These are the appointed feasts of ADONAI, the holy convocations which you are to proclaim at their appointed season." There are several critically important points in this verse. First, these are God-appointed seasons—sacred seasons for the community to come together to observe and celebrate. Second, ADONAI calls us together with him in this observance by telling us that we are to proclaim these days.

The book of Exodus is the story of God redeeming his people from Egypt. As a judgment on the false gods of Egypt, ADONAI sent ten plagues. The tenth and last plague was the death of every firstborn male. ADONAI told Moses that the Israelites were to slaughter a lamb and spread the blood on the doorframes of their homes. (Exodus 12:7) ADONAI's instructions continue in verse twelve:

"For I will go through the land of Egypt on that night and strike down every firstborn, both men and animals, and I will execute judgments against all the gods of Egypt. I am ADONAI. The blood will be a sign for you on the houses where you are. So there will be no plague among you to destroy you when I strike the land of Egypt. This day is to be a memorial for you. You are to keep it as a feast to ADONAI. Throughout your generations you are to keep it as an eternal ordinance."

It is good to remember that verse eleven states, "It is ADONAI's Passover." This was not a festival created by man, but one that was instituted by ADONAI. It is God's! God created it that we should always remember God's grace, mercy, love and redemptive purposes. Passover has been celebrated now for over three thousand years, and was observed by Yeshua every year of his life—first with his family, and later with his disciples. Passover was the occasion in which he took the cup and the *matzot,* and commanded his disciples (including us) to do this in remembrance of him. (Luke 22:7-20)

It is also worth noting that Yeshua said in Luke 22:18, "I will not drink again of the fruit of the vine until the kingdom of God comes." So there will be a day when we celebrate this meal with him!

When is Passover?

In instituting the Passover in Egypt, ADONAI told Moses and Aaron, "This month will mark the beginning of months for you; it is to be the first month of the year for you." (Exodus 12:2) According to Leviticus 23:6, "ADONAI's Passover begins at twilight on the fourteenth day of the first month." This naturally raises the question: what is the first month of the year?

The modern Hebrew calendar celebrates the civil New Year starting in the fall with the festival of *Rosh Hashanah* (the Feast of Trumpets). For example, the Jewish civil year of 5779 begins on the evening of September 9, 2018. The biblical Hebrew calendar, however, begins with the month of *Nisan* in the spring, according to ADONAI's instruction to Moses and Aaron.

It can be challenging to keep track of the date of Passover each year, because of the difference between the modern Gregorian calendar and the Hebrew one. The Gregorian calendar is strictly solar, with months that do not follow the phases of the moon. However the Hebrew calendar is both lunar and solar. It is lunar, in that each new month begins with a new moon. It is solar, in that a leap month is added every few years to keep months in their correct seasons. This means that there is not a consistent relationship between the Gregorian and Hebrew calendars. The following table demonstrates this issue in the dates of Passover for the years 2020 to 2025. (The Jewish day begins and ends at sunset.)

Year	First evening of Passover	Jewish Year
2020	Wednesday, April 8	5780
2021	Saturday, March 27	5781
2022	Friday, April 15	5782 *(Leap month added)*
2023	Wednesday, April 5	5783
2024	Monday, April 22	5784 *(Leap month added)*
2025	Saturday, April 12	5785

To follow the dating of Passover it is helpful to have a Jewish calendar. These can be found on the internet, or a printed version may be obtained from the website **www.messianicjewish.net**

Are Gentile Christians required to observe the feasts?

The feast days were given as part of God's covenant with Israel, a covenant that still exists today. (Romans chapters 10 and 11) For the sake of Jewish identity, expression, family and community, Jews will find it wise to observe them. However, according to Acts chapter fifteen and the Council of Jerusalem, Gentiles are not obligated to do so. Still, a case may be made that since Gentiles are grafted into the Olive Tree (Romans 11:11-24) they are called to share in the blessings ADONAI has given to Israel.

A second case for Gentiles observing the seven festivals of

Leviticus 23 is that these festivals are all about Jesus. They tell of his coming, his ministry and his future work yet to be fulfilled. Since these appointed times reveal God's plan of redemption, they provide a great benefit and foundation to the Christian faith for those who understand and experience them.

The Passover Seder

Seder means "order", so the Passover Seder is a ceremonial Passover meal which follows a specific order. The Passover Seder, which begins on the fifteenth day of the first month, consists of fifteen steps. The number fifteen reminds us of the fifteen Songs of Ascent, and of the Feast of Tabernacles *(Sukkot)* that occurs on the fifteenth day of the seventh month.

Fifteen also reminds us of the fifteen steps leading up to the Temple in Jerusalem from the south. Lastly, there are fifteen Hebrew words in the priestly blessing. (Numbers 6:22-27)

Thus, the number fifteen holds tremendous symbolism, reminding us of the meaning of Passover as we walk the pilgrim journey through the Seder.

The fifteen traditional steps vary from culture to culture. However, there is a common thread as participants are guided by the drinking of the four cups of wine, which come from the four "I will"s of Exodus 6:6.

The following Seder order is my own (Lon's) Messianic version. The fifteen steps are grouped by their respective places within the larger context of the Four Cups.

The Fifteen Steps of the Seder

The First Cup – "I Will Bring You Out"

1. Drinking the Cup of Sanctification *(Kadesh)*
2. Washing the Hands *(Urchatz)*
3. Dipping the Green Vegetable *(Karpas)*
4. Breaking the *Matzah*/Afikoman *(Yachatz)*

The Second Cup – "I Will Free You"

5. Telling the Story *(Miggid)*
   a. The Ten Plagues
   b. The Four Questions & Answers
   c. The Passover Lamb
   d. Singing "It Would Have Been Enough" *(Dayenu)*
   e. Drinking the Cup of Deliverance
6. Washing the Hands *(Rachtzah)*
7. Eating the *Matzah (Motzi)*
8. Eating the Bitter Herb *(Maror)*
9. Eating the Charoset and the Hillel Sandwich *(Korekh)*
10. Eating the Meal *(Shulchan Orekh)*
11. Tasting the Afikoman *(Tzafun)*

The Third Cup – "I Will Redeem You"

12. Drinking the Cup of Redemption *(Barekh)*
13. Singing the Songs of Praise *(Hallel)*

The Fourth Cup – "I Will Take You"

14. Drinking the Cup of Joy *(Nirtzah)*
15. Proclaiming "Next Year in Jerusalem" *(L'Shanah Haba'ah)*

The First Cup ⁸⁵

1. Drinking the Cup of Sanctification (Story, p. 27)

The first cup of wine James and John drink is known as the Cup of Sanctification. It corresponds to the first "I will" in Exodus 6:6, "I will bring you out." In the Exodus story this refers to God separating his people from the Egyptians. Today we call this the Cup of Sanctification, because sanctification is the process of being set apart, or separated, from evil. As it was with the Israelites, this is our first step to true freedom.

2. Washing of the Hands (Story, p. 27)

Although many commandments in the Torah do indeed concern health and personal hygiene, the practice of hand-washing before meals is purely symbolic. Thus, it may be done by every participant, or only by the leader. Jesus clashed with the Pharisees on this issue in Mark 7:3, because they expected it to occur before every meal. Jesus no doubt observed the ritual during the Seder, but did not adhere to the Pharisees' burdensome daily mandate. (This is important, in case anyone is concerned that Jesus ate his food with dirty hands.)

3. Dipping the Green Vegetable *(Karpas)* (Story, p. 28)

In this ritual, a vegetable like parsley is dipped into saltwater. Some maintain that the greenness of the vegetable represents the flourishing of the people of Israel prior to the famine which brought them to Egypt, and the saltwater represents the tears of slavery that came as a result. As we eat, we are to enter in fully to this suffering and sadness,

---

⁸⁵ For more about the First Cup, and the first "I will" statement from Exodus, see page 114.

as if it were our own.

The reader may also be reminded of Jesus' self-identification with the symbol of the "green tree" in Ezekiel 20:47. (Luke 23:31) This is one of several messianic claims where Jesus compares himself to a flourishing plant, such as a tree or vine, to symbolize the new life he comes to bring to the world.

4. Breaking the *Matzah*/Afikoman (Story, p. 26-30)

Matzah is the Hebrew word for "unleavened bread". *Matzah* serves as a central element to the Passover Seder, as it was specifically commanded by God in the celebration of the festival, both in the Exodus story and in Leviticus. In the Exodus story, the Israelites are commanded to eat their bread without yeast, to help speed their departure from Egypt. Thus, one of the primary features of Passover is to eat bread for eight days with no yeast. (Exodus chapter 12)

Jesus, at the Last Supper, equates the Passover *matzah* to his own body, about to be broken. This is a highly appropriate analogy, since yeast, or leaven, which represents sin elsewhere in Scripture, is absent from the bread, and sin is absent from Jesus. It's also fascinating to note that a typical sheet of *matzah* is both "pierced" and "striped", evoking the prophecy in Isaiah 53:5, that the messiah would be "pierced because of our transgressions", and that "by his stripes we are healed."

Another way Jesus is symbolized in the *matzah* is in the ritual of the Afikoman. (See "11. Tasting the Afikoman" on page 106.)

100

The Second Cup 86

5. Telling the Story (Story, p. 37)

At its core, Passover is a story. Not only that, it is one of the foundational narratives that helps define the great themes of Scripture. This is the part of the Seder where participants take turns reading portions of the story aloud, so we never forget the great works of God in the past, for the sake of the present and the future.

5a. The Ten Plagues (Story, p. 37)

Exodus chapters seven through twelve recount the ten plagues to which God subjected the Egyptians. In each case, the land of Goshen (where the Israelites live) is exempted from the misery. The only exception is the tenth plague, which does not exempt them geographically or ethnically, but on the basis of their obedience to God's instructions.

1. **Blood**—The Nile River turns to blood
2. **Frogs**—The land is overwhelmed by frogs
3. **Bugs**—The land swarms with insects
4. **Wild Animals**—Beasts of all kinds ravage the land
5. **Pestilence**—Disease wipes out domestic animals
6. **Boils**—Every man and beast is infected with painful boils
7. **Hail**—Hail kills every plant and unsheltered creature
8. **Locusts**—Locusts devour everything left by the hail
9. **Darkness**—The sun, moon and all kindled lights are dark
10. **Death of the Firstborn**—Moses warns that the Angel of Death will take the firstborn male of every family, except in those homes where God's instructions—to slaughter a lamb and paint its blood on their doorframes—are followed.

---

[86] For more about the Second Cup, and the second "I will" statement, see page 115.

5b. The Four Questions & Answers (Story, p. 38)

One of the key moments in the Seder is called the Four Questions, where the reasoning behind various aspects of the meal is explained to the participants. The over-arching "theme question" is: Why is this night different from all other nights? The four questions below are intended explore this theme question in detail.

1. On all other nights we eat leavened products and *matzah*, why on this night do we eat only *matzah*?
2. On all other nights we eat all vegetables, why on this night do we eat only bitter herbs?
3. On all other nights, we don't dip our food even once, why on this night do we dip twice?
4. On all other nights we eat sitting or reclining, why on this night do we only recline?

The questions are answered with variations on the assertion that *we ourselves* were slaves. By celebrating in this way, we enter in fully to the plight, the bitterness and ultimate joy of our ancestors. Believers in Jesus experience an additional degree of specialness on this night, because it's the night he commanded us to eat and drink in remembrance of him.

5c. The Passover Lamb (Story, p. 37)

When the Angel of Death passed through Egypt, its mission was to see that one death was dealt on every household. Although this is harsh, it was the final straw of justice for a kingdom that had repeatedly mocked and rejected the One True God. We sometimes refer to him as a "God of second chances", but this was Egypt's *tenth chance*.

This occasion also created a test of faith for the Israelites. Each family now had the opportunity to "show" the angel that death had already been achieved for that household, and no further judgment was necessary. Thus, the family with the blood of a lamb on its doorposts would be "passed over".

A lamb was required, but it couldn't be just any lamb. It had to be a male, one year old or less, without defect. The chosen creature could not be old, or lame, or sick, and thus close to death. It had to be a true sacrifice—a real loss. To intensify that loss, the lamb had to live with the family for four days, allowing them to bond with it like a pet.

That makes two important criteria for the lamb: (1) It had to be perfect, and (2) it had to be loved. Both of these features make it a valuable animal. In other words, this act had to mean something. If it hadn't, no faith would be required at all.

5d. "It Would Have Been Enough" (Dayenu) (Story, p. 38)

Dayenu is one of the liveliest songs traditionally sung during a Passover Seder. The Hebrew word means "It would have been enough" and reminds participants to be thankful for every work of God in their lives, instead of anxiously awaiting the next one. God expresses this same principle to the Apostle Paul, when God tells him "My grace is sufficient for you." (2 Corinthians 12:9)

John utters the word *Dayenu* at the end of Part I as an expression of this kind of faith. Although he would prefer James to live, and could imagine many potential blessings as a result, he thanks God for the fullness of his life up to that point, no matter what happens.

When sung in full, the song contains fifteen verses (a very significant number – see page 97) which follow the same format:

Had God brought us out of Egypt
But not executed judgment on the Egyptians
It would have been enough (Dayenu)!

The fifteen verses list the works of God in three groups of five, as follows:

Five Stanzas of Liberation

1. God brought us out of Egypt
2. God executed judgment on the Egyptians
3. God executed judgment on their gods
4. God slayed their firstborn
5. God gave us their wealth

Five Stanzas of Miracles

6. God split the sea for us
7. God led us through on dry land
8. God drowned our oppressors
9. God provided for our needs for 40 years in the wilderness
10. God fed us manna

Five Stanzas of Being with God

11. God gave us the Sabbath
12. God led us to Mount Sinai
13. God gave us the Torah
14. God brought us to the Land of Israel
15. God built the Temple for us

Messianic versions of the song may add new verses that refer to the fulfillment of these events, such as the incarnation, life, death and resurrection of Yeshua (Jesus) the Messiah, the sending of the *Ruakh HaKodesh* (Holy Spirit), and the establishment of the New Covenant.

5e. The Cup of Deliverance (Story, p. 39)

Also known as the Cup of Judgment (against the Egyptians), the drinking of this cup commemorates the Israelites' moment of freedom from slavery. It serves as a climax to the Story of Deliverance, which takes the participant from the infancy of Moses to the parting of the Red Sea. In the *Dayenu,* the story is extended even further into the future.

The theme of all the activities leading up to the Cup of Deliverance is the participants' willing embrace of the experience of slavery. Thus, when the story recounts their deliverance, we can fully identify with that freedom, especially through the work of Jesus in our hearts.

6. Washing the Hands (Story, p. 46)

For a second time, participants wash their hands, or the leader may wash his or her hands on behalf of everyone present.

7. Eating the *Matzah* (Story, p. 46)

Before introducing the *maror* and the *charoset,* another piece of *matzah* is eaten. In some modern Seders, a participant will take a sheet of *matzah,* and break it into five pieces. The first is eaten plain, the second is eaten with the *maror* spread on top, the third with the *charoset,* and the fourth and fifth are used to assemble the Hillel sandwich (see commentary note below.)

8. Eating the Bitter Herb *(Maror)* (Story, p. 47)

Maror is the "bitter herb", usually horseradish, which evokes the bitterness of slavery in Egypt. To take too much, as James does, causes the eyes to water and really clears the sinuses.

9. Eating the Charoset and the Hillel Sandwich (Story, p. 48)

Charoset is a sweet concoction often comprised of chopped apples, nuts, red wine, cinnamon and honey. Its texture and color is said to represent the mortar which Jewish slaves used to make bricks in Egypt. In the meal, it serves to chase away the bitterness of the *maror,* which is consumed immediately prior.

One striking feature of *charoset* is its role in making the famous Hillel sandwich. A Hillel sandwich is composed of two pieces of *matzah,* with *maror* and *charoset* in between. The effect is startling and delicious, as the sweet mixes with the bitter. Although this sandwich is not featured in the Story, it is referenced indirectly by John's need to transport the *maror* and *charoset* in the same jar, and James' joke that the two might actually taste good together.

It is doubtful that *charoset* was part of the Seder meal during the time of James and John.

10. Eating the Meal (Story, p. 48)

Finally, two-thirds of the way through the ritual, dinner is served. Although this is the most casual portion of the Seder, it is also rich with symbolism. The original entrée of the meal was the lamb, which carried multiple layers of meaning for the Israelites escaping Egypt. The fact that God focused his commandments so carefully on the communal eating of this meal should remind us of the importance of eating together as a community. This carries forward into the way we, as believers today, receive Communion, or the Eucharist, together as one body.

Traditional food served for the Passover meal includes *matzah* ball soup, gefilte fish, chopped liver, and macaroons for dessert. Although there is no prescriptive menu for the occasion, the foods must be chosen carefully, since the eight-day festival of Passover prohibits the consumption of yeast. (*Matzah* pizza, anyone?)

11. Tasting the Afikoman (Story, p. 48)

The ceremonial *Afikoman* may or may not have been instituted by the time of James and John. But it is a wonderful symbol of the redemptive themes inherent in the Passover Seder. Three sheets of *matzah* are placed together on a plate, then the middle one is pulled out and broken in half. The larger half, now called the *Afikoman,* is wrapped in a cloth and hidden away.

After the meal, the children look all over the house to find it. The one who succeeds is then rewarded, usually with money. Finally, the recovered *matzah* is enjoyed as if it were a dessert, apropos to the word *Afikoman,* which translates "that which comes after."

The *Afikoman* is a clear symbol of the Trinity, and Jesus' redemptive role therein. As the second (or "middle") member of the Trinity, God the Son was willingly removed from his place of divine glory, broken on the cross, and hidden from sight (buried in a tomb.) But he was not hidden forever, because in his resurrection he is revealed again, and all who now find him are rewarded, in this case with eternal life.

This symbolism was initiated by Jesus when he picked up the *Afikoman,* immediately before the Cup of Redemption, and equated it to his own body, broken and given for us. (See "From the Gospels" on page 135.)

The Third Cup [87]

12. Drinking the Cup of Redemption (Story, p. 53)

Between the Cup of Deliverance and the Cup of Redemption, James and John find the reconciliation they both need so desperately. James is delivered from spiritual bondage by his confession of bitterness, and redeemed by the blood of Jesus, represented in the

---

[87] For more about the Third Cup, and the third "I will" statement from Exodus, see page 116.

Third Cup.

Thinking back to the Exodus, we know that the Israelites were fully delivered by the time the tenth plague was complete. But they were not yet redeemed. They were still in the land of captivity. If they had stayed long enough, they may well have found themselves enslaved again. The Third Cup represents the passage through the Red Sea, and the birth of a nation fully separated from its oppressor.

We are not so different today. We can live lives of confession (the baptism of John – Acts 18:25) which may break the bonds of sin for a time. Or we can be fully redeemed by the blood of the Lamb, pass through the waters (the baptism of Jesus – Matthew 28:19) and leave our lives of sin behind us once and for all.

This is the meaning of the Third Cup—the Cup of Redemption. When Jesus came to this moment in the Last Supper, after having equated the *Afikoman* to his broken body, he said "This is my blood, poured out for you." He was fulfilling the promise, once and for all, to redeem us out of our selfish lives and into his abundant life. And if the Son sets us free, we will be free indeed. (John 8:36)

13. Singing the Songs of Praise *(Hallel)* (Story, p. 54)

After the Cup of Redemption, James and John sing songs found in Psalms 113 to 118. These psalms were ritually chanted in the Temple while the Passover lambs were being slain. Many well-known expressions of spirit and truth are found in these songs:

113:3 "From the rising of the sun to its going down the Name of ADONAI is to be praised."

115:1 "Not to us, ADONAI, not to us, but to Your Name be the glory— because of Your love and Your faithfulness."

116:1-2 "I love ADONAI, for He hears my voice, my cries. Because He has turned His ear to me, I will call on Him all my days.

116:13-14 "I will lift up the cup of salvation, and call on the Name of ADONAI. I will fulfill my vows to ADONAI in the presence of all His people."

118:1 "Praise ADONAI, for He is good, for His lovingkindness endures forever."

118:14-16 "ADONAI is my strength and song, and He has become my salvation. Shouts of joy and victory are in the tents of the righteous: "ADONAI's right hand is mighty! ADONAI's right hand is lifted high! ADONAI's right hand is mighty!"

118:21-26 (excerpts) "You have answered me and have become my salvation. The stone the builders rejected has become the capstone. This is the day that ADONAI has made! Let us rejoice and be glad in it! Hosanna! Please, ADONAI, save now! Blessed is He who comes in the Name of ADONAI. We bless you from the House of ADONAI." [88]

The Fourth Cup [89]

14. Drinking the Cup of Joy (Story, p. 54)

Some believers, when celebrating Passover, choose not to drink the fourth of the Four Cups. In Matthew 26:29, Jesus says, "I will never

---

[88] This passage in the *Hallel* is quoted by the followers of Jesus welcoming him to Jerusalem before his crucifixion (The "triumphal entry" on Palm Sunday.) The term "House of ADONAI" refers to the Temple in Jerusalem.

[89] For more about the Fourth Cup, and the fourth "I will" statement from Exodus, see page 117.

drink of this fruit of the vine from now on, until that day when I drink it anew with you in My Father's kingdom." This is the moment where his disciples were expecting to drink the Fourth Cup—the Cup of Joy—but Jesus demurred.

He had just equated the wine in the Third Cup to his own blood, which he would spill the very next day to redeem us all. By stopping there, he effectively paused the Seder for thousands of years, allowing us to live out the fullness of that Third Cup, called the Cup of Redemption. Thus, one could say we're living in the "Age of the Third Cup". But when the Kingdom has fully come, it will be time for all followers of Jesus to drink the Fourth Cup together. This is what Revelation 19:7 calls the Wedding Supper of the Lamb, and the body of believers is his shining bride.

15. Proclaiming "Next Year in Jerusalem"

At the very heart of Passover is the hope of the Promised Land. God did not set us free simply to scatter to the winds, but to gather us in a place of worship and blessing.

Unfortunately, God's people scattered anyway. Some were conquered and dragged away, others left of their own volition. And now we are spread all across the world. But there is a unifying hope, as everyone who assembles on the eve of Passover cries together with one voice, "Next year in Jerusalem!"

Although we have been redeemed by the blood of the Lamb of God, we are still in exile. But one day, we will drink the Fourth Cup once and for all with Jesus, at the Marriage Supper of the Lamb. It may be far in the future, or it may be near. But we are called to live every day in the spirit of Revelation 22:20, proclaiming "Amen! Come, Lord Jesus!"

In the story, the seder is interrupted before the Fourth Cup, which means that James and John are unable to share that proclamation together. John had celebrated the Seder every year of his life, and had always finished it, until now. The ending must have hung in the air like an unresolved melody.

Perhaps the phrase *"L'shanah haba'ah b'Yerushalayim"*—"Next year in Jerusalem"—echoes in John's mind as he chases after James, and observes his final testament. And perhaps these are the words John writes in the sand, to bring closure in his own mind to the last Seder of James.

Passover Seder Traditions

There are some biblical commands regarding the celebration of Passover, and there are many traditions based purely on culture. Presented here are some of the most prominent traditions, and a general idea of how they have been observed in different eras and cultures. First, a quick explanation of the five "eras", represented in this table as five columns, with corresponding icons.

 First Passover in Egypt (Approx. 1300 BC)
These are one-time practices, which did not all carry forward into the annual traditions of Passover.

 Temple-Based Judaism (Before AD 70)
This is "biblical" Judaism (through the time of Jesus) based around the Tabernacle and 1st and 2nd Temples.

 Post-Temple Judaism (AD 70 – Present)
This is "rabbinic" Judaism, based on the Torah and Talmud, after the destruction of the 2nd Temple.

 Messianic Jews & Gentiles (1967 – Present)
Followers of Jesus who identify with Jewish heritage and practice. Focus here is on the modern movement.

 Gentile Christian Church (Approx. AD 30 – Present)
Those who do not celebrate Passover, but observe the cup and the bread as a sacrament instituted by Jesus.

Passover Traditions From Age to Age

	Historical			Modern	
	First Passover in Egypt (~1300 BC)	Temple-Based Judaism (Before AD 70)	Post-Temple Judaism (AD 70 – Present)	Messianic Jews & Gentiles (1967 – Present)	Gentile Christian Church (~AD 30 – Present)
Lamb slaughtered at home — *Exodus 12:7, 22*	●				
Meal eaten in haste — *Exodus 12:11*	●				
Lamb's blood on doorposts — *Exodus 12:7, 22 - Some Jewish sects still do this*	●				
Lamb selected 10th day of 1st month — *Exodus 12:3-6*	●	●			
Lamb sacrificed & roasted — *Exodus 12:8a - Some traditions eat lamb, some do not*	●	●			
Lamb not cooked in water — *Exodus 12:9*	●	●			
No lamb meat left until morning — *Exodus 12:10*	●	●			
Passover "when you enter the land" — *Exodus 12:25, Joshua 5:10*		●	●		
Passover to be a lasting ordinance — *Exodus 12:3-6*	●	●	●	●	
Centered on house & family — *Exodus 12:46a*	●	●	●	●	
Feast of Unleavened Bread Observed — *Exodus 12:15-20, Joshua 5:11*	●	●	●	●	
House cleaned, all yeast removed — *Exodus 12:8c*	●	●	●	●	
Bitter herbs — *Exodus 12:8b*	●	●	●	●	
None of the lamb's bones broken — *Exodus 12:46b*	●	●	●	●	
Exodus story told to children — *Exodus 12:26-27*	●	●	●	●	
Singing of the Hallel — *Psalm 113-118*	●	●	●	●	
Four cups of wine — *Extra-biblical; prescribed in the Mishnah*	●		●	●	
Cup & bread "in remembrance" of Jesus — *Luke 22:17, 19*	●			●	●

The Four Cups and the Four "I Wills"

The order of the Passover Seder is primarily structured around the "I will" promises of Exodus chapter six. The first four of these promises corresponds to the traditional four cups of the Seder.

"I am ADONAI, and I will bring you out from under the yoke of the Egyptians. I will free you from being slaves to them, and I will redeem you with an outstretched arm and with mighty acts of judgment. I will take you as my own people, and I will be your God. Then you will know that I am ADONAI your God, who brought you out from under the yoke of the Egyptians. And I will bring you to the land I swore with uplifted hand to give to Abraham, to Isaac and to Jacob. I will give it to you as a possession. I am ADONAI." (Exodus 6:6-8)

The four cups of wine are symbolic of the four "I wills" (along with the corresponding redemptive verbs) of verses six and seven:

1. **"I will bring you out** from under the yoke of the Egyptians."
2. **"I will free you** from being slaves to them."
3. **"I will redeem you** with an outstretched arm."
4. **"I will take you** as my own people."

The First Cup – "I Will Bring You Out"

The first "I will" corresponds to the First Cup, or the Cup of Sanctification, which begins the Passover Seder meal. It is a recognition that there is a separation between the time in Egypt and the time out of Egypt. There is division between slavery and freedom, and consequently a difference between secular time and sacred time. [90] Just as the Sabbath was set apart as sacred time, the Israelites were now being "set apart" from Egypt, into their destiny and identity as a

---

[90] Nahum M. Sarna and Chaim Potok eds., *The JPS Torah Commentary: Exodus* (Jerusalem, The Jewish Publication Society, 1989), 15.

nation devoted to ADONAI, as a sacred nation and a priesthood for all the nations.

Within this "I will" is the promise of a calling into that covenant relationship, which is the promise of redemption, of being set free from the chains of the world. The Israelites were to live differently than the world lived, in order to bring the light of God to the world. Israel was set apart to reveal God's glory and his redemptive purpose to all peoples. They were to bring the righteousness and justice of God's kingdom to the earth. Jesus affirms this when he cleanses the Temple, quoting Isaiah 56:7, "My house will be called a house of prayer for all nations." (Mark 11:17)

The Second Cup – "I Will Free You"

The second "I will" correlates to the Second Cup of Passover, which is called the Cup of Judgment. This represents the judgment on Egypt for enslaving God's people and for worshipping false gods. (Exodus 7:14-11:10)

The first and the tenth plagues involved blood, perhaps to mirror the recent mass murder of Israelite newborns. The judgments started and ended with a definitive declaration by God that these were intended as judgments upon Egypt, and the false gods of Egypt.

In the plagues, God symbolically confronts the false gods of Egypt: *Uatchit* the fly god, *Apis* the bull god, *Hathor* the cow god, and *Sekhmet* the goddess of epidemics. The gods of water, land and sky are all called to account and one by one they fail to protect the Egyptian people from disaster. The series builds until the ninth plague, which challenges *Ra* (the supreme god, or sun god), and *Thoth* (the moon god), as darkness covers the land for three days. Pharaoh, as a god himself, is targeted in the tenth and final plague—

the death of the firstborn. [91]

The Third Cup – "I Will Redeem You"

The third "I will" corresponds to the Cup of Redemption. This is
the cup which is taken after the meal, and is the cup to which Jesus
referred in Luke 22:20. This cup is essentially the heart of the Passover
celebration, which can be seen not only from Jesus' comments but
from the meaning of the Hebrew word for "redeem". That word is
go'el (go-AYL, "kinsman-redeemer").

This biblical concept is most famously presented in the book of
Ruth, where Boaz becomes the kinsman-redeemer to Naomi and Ruth
the Moabitess. (Ruth 4:1-12) In other passages God is called the
"Redeemer, the Holy One of Israel", (Isaiah 41:14, 48:17, 49:7, 54:5)
"Israel's King and Redeemer" (Isaiah 43:14) and "your Savior, your
Redeemer". (Isaiah 49:26) Also, Job proclaims, "I know that my
Redeemer lives, and in the end, He will stand on earth." (Job 19:25)

Other obligations of the kinsman-redeemer include the duty to
redeem a relative if he had sold himself into slavery, (Leviticus 25:48-
49) to re-purchase the property of a relative who had to sell it because
of poverty, to avenge the blood of a relative, to marry a brother's
widow in order to have a son on his brother's behalf, (Deuteronomy
25:5-6) and to receive restitution if an injured relative dies. (Numbers
5:8)

It should also be noted that the divine work of redemption is done
"with an outstretched arm" which symbolizes strength and power,

---

[91] The authors are not implying that the God of Moses defeated actual gods of Egypt,
as if they were real, but weak. (This is a variant of monotheism common among
ancients, called henotheism.) Rather, the reality is that these gods were pure figments
of imagination and cultural manipulation. As such, no divine power was available to
the Egyptians to counter that of the Almighty God.

and thus is used metaphorically of God's own mighty deeds. [92] God, not Moses, is explicitly identified as the one responsible for bringing the people out. This is stated repeatedly throughout the Exodus story, such that no mistake can be made that this is a redemptive act of God, and not simply the work of a great leader. [93] This fact was made plain to both the Israelites and the Egyptians.

The Fourth Cup – "I Will Take You"

The fourth "I will" corresponds to the fourth and final cup of the Seder, called the Cup of Joy or the Cup of Rejoicing. The JPS Torah Commentary illuminates the meaning of "I will take you":

This declaration prefigures the covenant that is to be established at Sinai. The phraseology suggests the institution of marriage, a familiar biblical metaphor for the relationship between God and Israel. The first two verbs, "to take" and "to be (someone's)" are both used in connection with matrimony; the second is also characteristic covenant language. Similarly, the Hebrew term for a covenant is also used for the bond of marriage. [94]

The language, the words, and the meaning are all relational—marriage-relational, covenant-relational. The liberation of the Israelites brought them into their covenant relationship as given to Abraham, Isaac and Jacob. ADONAI set them free for the express purpose of establishing a relationship with him—an eternal relationship—to which ADONAI and Abraham had bound themselves. Thus the redemptive history and the identities of God and Abraham were forever bound together. Sam Nadler points out that God made

---

[92] Sarna, 32

[93] J. H. Hertz, *Pentateuch and Haftorahs* (London: Soncino Press, 1971), 233.

[94] Sarna, 32

two promises:

1. The promise of his presence: "I will not fail you or forsake you." (Joshua 1:5)

2. The promise of his purpose: "Now we know that all things work together for good for those who love God, who are called according to His purpose." (Romans 8:28) [95]

There are three more "I will"s with a concluding "I am." The essence of the first four "I will"s is found in the definitive statement in verse seven: "I will be your God." The God who revealed himself to Abraham and now to Moses will fulfill his promise to be their God, and with the sixth "I will" God now declares, "I will bring you to the Land" and "I will give it to you as a possession." Earlier, in verse four, God affirmed his commitment to Abraham to bring them to the Promised Land, and now adds that he will also give it to them.

Not only was God bringing them out and setting them free, but he was fulfilling his promise and bringing them to the Land. He did this so that they could now live in it and possess it, not as foreigners and aliens but as citizens of their own nation. This was to be a nation not like other nations, but one living in a covenant relationship with God.

God's promise, and the fulfillment of that promise, is celebrated in the first four "I will"s. In these four, God set his people free and takes them as a bride. In the three subsequent "I will"s, God dwells with his people.

The fifth statement is, "I will be your God." This expresses God's intention to come and dwell with us. God has bound himself to humankind in the Abrahamic covenant, and the phraseology of the "I

---

[95] Sam Nadler, *Messiah in the Feasts of Israel* (Charlotte: Word of Messiah Ministries, 2010), 32.

will"s reveals the depth of that relationship. It is comparable to the life-long relationship of marriage—an intimate, personal commitment.

In Exodus 40:1, after ADONAI gives detailed instructions on the construction of the Tabernacle, he tells Moses to set it up on the first day of the first month of the second year. If the first year in the desert was the year of engagement, then the establishment of the Tabernacle was the wedding, because this is when God came to dwell—to "tabernacle"—with them.

This language is also found in the opening statements of the gospel of John, "and the Word became flesh and [tabernacled] among us." (John1:14)

John goes on to say, "We looked upon His glory, the glory of the one and only from the Father, full of grace and truth." This glory is the same glory that filled the Tabernacle, when "the cloud covered the Tent of Meeting, and the glory of ADONAI filled the Tabernacle. Moses was unable to enter into the Tent of Meeting, because the cloud resided there and the glory of ADONAI filled the Tabernacle." (Exodus 40:34-35) God's presence and majesty—his *kavod*—was now dwelling with them.

This occurred again at the time of King Solomon. The Temple construction was finished and the Ark of the Covenant was brought from the City of David to the Temple. The Temple was dedicated in the seventh month at the time of the Feast of Tabernacles *(Sukkot)* which they celebrated for seven days. When the Ark arrived at the Holy Place, "the cloud filled the House of ADONAI so that the *kohanim* [96] could not stand to minister because of the cloud, for the glory of ADONAI filled the House of ADONAI." (I Kings 8:10)

---

[96] priests

The rejoicing was so great that they extended the holiday seven more days, for a total of fourteen days. This is the meaning of the fifth "I will": that God in his glory has come to dwell with his people and take them as his bride.

As majestic as it may be, the indwelling of God in the times of Moses or Solomon is designed to point toward the ultimate incarnation ("coming in the flesh") of the Messiah Jesus. This is why John borrows so much from "tabernacle" imagery. He describes how Jesus was born, lived and died just like us, and thus serves as the fulfillment of the dwelling of God amongst his people.

The Festivals

To be a Christian, by definition, is to be a "little Christ". To be like Jesus. This is what Jesus means when he calls us to be disciples, and to make disciples. A genuine Christians is a person who strives to walk, talk, think and act just like Jesus would, if he were in our shoes.

The New Testament is the divinely inspired guide for all those who aspire to discipleship. The Gospels tell us the story of Jesus' ministry, death, resurrection and ascension. The Acts of the Apostles recounts the story of Pentecost and the early years of the Church. And the Epistles explain in greater detail what these stories mean for us, and how to make the kinds of choices in our lives that Jesus might make.

However, the New Testament is only a portion of what God has given us to understand the life of a disciple. After all, Jesus didn't have any of it. He read and studied and lived by the Hebrew Scriptures—the Law of Moses, the Prophets, and the Writings. [97] The writers of the New Testament were all, or nearly all, Jewish like Jesus. And if there is any doubt about the importance of the Old Testament in understanding the New, note that the latter quotes the former over 800 times. If one were to include indirect quotations and allusions the number would be in the thousands. In short, the entire New Testament is drawn from the concepts, prophecies and history of the Old.

One major example of the patterns of the Old Testament providing a framework for the New is that of the Jewish Festivals, especially the seven Levitical Festivals outlined in Leviticus 23.

The festivals provide a yearly life cycle which also affects the way

---

[97] Or, in Hebrew: *Torah, Nevi'im, Ketuvim,* the abbreviation of which produces the name of the Jewish equivalent to the Old Testament: *The Tanakh.*

practitioners live on a daily basis. It is a way of living that reminds us never to forget our salvation and the goodness of God. As the Lord instructs us in Deuteronomy 6:10-12: "When the Lord your God brings you into the land he swore to your fathers ... then when you eat and are satisfied, *be careful that you do not forget the Lord,* who brought you out of Egypt, out of the land of slavery."

When we are grounded in our historical Biblical roots, not only by our knowledge but also but our pattern of living and as a way of life it helps to preserve us so that we do not forget. In celebrating Resurrection Sunday it takes us back to the resurrection of Jesus but we must not stop there, for the resurrection is rooted in Passover. We must continue back to the foundation of Resurrection Sunday which is our Abrahamic roots and the covenant God made with him. As Paul says "Abraham is the father of all that believe."[98] We must not forget our historical roots lest we drift astray.

The Seven Levitical Festivals

The Lord said to Moses, "Speak to the Israelites and say to them 'These are my appointed feasts, the appointed feasts of the Lord, which you are to proclaim as sacred assemblies.'"[99]

The Seven Levitical Festivals are found in Exodus, Leviticus, Numbers and Deuteronomy but Leviticus 23 serves well as a primary source. As verse four proclaims, "These are the Lord's appointed feasts, the sacred assemblies you are to proclaim at their times." They do not belong to any group of humans, or to humanity in general. Instead, they belong to God. And we are called to enter into them as we proclaim them to the world.

Even some who are conversant with the Jewish calendar may be unfamiliar with a few of the festivals listed below. This is because the

---

[98] Romans 4:11
[99] Leviticus 23:1-2

Passover is conventionally viewed and celebrated as a single eight-day festival, but in the Torah it is outlined as three distinct times: Passover (one day), Unleavened Bread (the following seven days), and First Fruits (one day, within the seven days of Unleavened Bread). Furthermore, some of the more popular holidays, such as Hanukkah and Purim, were instituted after the Torah was written.

Jesus would have identified deeply with all the festivals, from both a community perspective and an individual perspective. Jesus knew that it would be through his life, ministry, suffering, death, resurrection, ascension and promise to return that he would fulfill each and every one of the seven festivals.

Below is a brief overview of the original Seven Levitical Festivals. Further detail on Passover and the Feast of Weeks (Shavu'ot) is provided in a later section.

Passover (Pesach) and the New Year

"The Lord's Passover begins at twilight on the fourteenth day of the first month." [100]

The biblical new year starts in the spring as commanded by God in Exodus 12:2, "This month is to be for you the first month ... of your year." None of the months had names at this point. (Today Judaism calls the first month Nisan.) Passover [101] begins on the fifteenth day of the first month.

The importance of this cannot be overstated. In Joshua, the Lord had the Israelites enter the Promised Land at the start of the new year. In fact the first thing that the Israelites did once in the land, after crossing the Jordan and setting up the twelve standing stones, was to celebrate the

---

[100] Leviticus 23:5

[101] *Pesach* in Hebrew which means "to spring, jump or pass over" something.

123

Passover. [102]

Passover was also important to Mary and Joseph, the parents of Jesus. Luke 2:41 records that, "Every year [Jesus'] parents went to Jerusalem for the Feast of Passover." It was only a requirement that Joseph go but since both of his parents went it would be reasonable to assume that they took the children and travelled with many friends and relatives. [103] Jesus probably celebrated Passover in Jerusalem all of his adult life and many of his childhood years. He also stated that he eagerly desired [104] to celebrate the Passover with his disciples. [105]

Aside from the Gospels, allusions to Passover are found all throughout the New Testament. The book of Revelation, for example, contains many references to the Exodus-Passover event when referring to the Song of Moses and in referring to Jesus as the Lamb.

Unleavened Bread (Matzah)

"On the fifteenth day of that month the Lord's Feast of Unleavened Bread begins; for seven days you must eat bread made without yeast." [106]

The feast of unleavened bread begins on the day after Passover and lasts for seven days – from the evening of the sixteenth day until the evening of the twenty-second day. Biblically, Passover and Unleavened Bread are two separate festivals but are commonly called the eight days of Passover in Judaism today.

The time of Unleavened Bread is fairly self-explanatory, as it is focused on the avoidance of leaven, or yeast, in the household. This is the reason for the ritual eating of *matzah,* or unleavened bread. Multiple references to this in the New Testament use yeast as a metaphor for sin. This is especially significant when Jesus compares the *matzah* to his own

---

[102] Joshua 4:19-5:15

[103] Joachim, Jeremias, *Jerusalem in the Time of Jesus*

[104] Luke 22:15

[105] Luke 22:7-22, Matthew 26:17-30, Mark 14:12-26, John 13:1-30

[106] Leviticus 23:6

body, which is "broken" for us. Just as there was no yeast in the bread, there was no sin in his body.

First Fruits (Yom HaBikkurim)

"Speak to the Israelites and say to them: 'When you enter the land I am going to give you and you reap its harvest, bring to the priest a sheaf of the first grain you harvest. He is to wave the sheaf before the Lord so it will be accepted on your behalf; the priest is to wave it on the day after the Sabbath." [107]

The feast of First Fruits begins the day after the Passover Sabbath. The Pharisees, and later Rabbinic Judaism, interpreted this to mean the day after Passover (the first day of Unleavened Bread), but the Sadducees and others believed it occurred on the day after the regular Sabbath during or after Passover. The latter interpretation causes First Fruits to always fall on the Sunday within the eight days of Passover/Unleavened bread.

This is important because Sunday, or the first day of the week, signifies new beginnings and relates to the number eight as a number of dedication. As we will see further down, this interpretation also causes Shavu'ot to always fall on a Sunday.

Feast of Weeks (Shavu'ot / Pentecost)

"From the day after the Sabbath the day you brought the sheaf of the wave offering, count off seven full weeks. Count off fifty days up to the day after the seventh Sabbath and then present an offering of new grain to the Lord." [108]

After the festival of First Fruits comes the counting of the fifty days, called the Counting of the Omer (explained in more detail in a later section) which leads up to the festival of Shavu'ot. This festival is also known as the "latter first fruits" because the fruit of the wheat harvest was brought in and waved before the Lord in worship and thanksgiving.

---

[107] Leviticus 23:10-11
[108] Leviticus 23:15-16

Barney Kasdan, a Messianic Jewish Rabbi, writes in his excellent book, *God's Appointed Times*: "Shavu'ot is designated as a time of thanksgiving for the early harvest. God's faithfulness in providing the early wheat harvest increases hopefulness for an abundant fall harvest (at Sukkot).[109]

Also known as Pentecost, this festival is related to the giving of the law to Moses at Mt. Sinai in the third month.[110] It takes place in the third month of the Jewish calendar, which is known as Sivan and starts in late May or early June. Since Shavu'ot, or Pentecost, is the primary focus of this book, it is described in much greater detail in other sections.

Feast of Trumpets (Rosh Hashanah / Yom Teruah)

"On the first day of the seventh month you are to have a day of rest, a sacred assembly commemorated with trumpet blasts. Do no regular work but present an offering made to the Lord by fire." [111]

The Feast of Trumpets celebrates the Jewish civil new year and should not be confused with the biblical new year that starts in the Spring. Scripture is brief on the subject, but establishes the Feast of Trumpets as a time of regathering, initiating the ten days of preparation for the Day of Atonement. The trumpet blasts are considered the "wake-up call; an alarm to call us to our appointed time." [112]

Day of Atonement (Yom Kippur)

"The tenth day of this seventh month is the Day of Atonement. Hold a sacred assembly and deny yourselves, and present an offering made to the Lord by fire. Do no work on that day, because it is the Day of Atonement, when atonement is made for you before the Lord your God. Anyone who does not deny himself on that day must be cut off from his people. I will destroy from among his people anyone who does any work

---

[109] Kasdan, 52
[110] Exodus 19:1
[111] Leviticus 23:23-25
[112] Kasdan, 65

on that day. You shall do no work at all. This is to be a lasting ordinance for the generations to come, wherever you live. It is a sabbath of rest for you, and you must deny yourselves. From the evening of the ninth day of the month until the following evening you are to observe your sabbath." [113]

The Day of Atonement is considered the holiest day of the year with all thirty-four verses of Leviticus chapter sixteen being devoted to the explicit way in which it was to be observed. This was the day when the high priest would enter the Holy of Holies to make "atonement for himself, his household and the whole community of Israel." [114]

Kasdan writes: "Yom Kippur is considered the logical extension of what was started at Rosh Hashanah. In fact, the ten days between Rosh Hashanah and Yom Kippur take on their own holy significance. They're called the Yomim Nora'im, The Days of Awe. Traditional Jews, as well as many non-traditional Jews, spend these days looking inward, seeing how their inner life might be more pleasing to God. Personal relationships are evaluated; forgiveness and restitution are offered where needed. Reconciliation is attempted." [115]

Feast of Tabernacles (Sukkot)

"The Lord said to Moses, 'Say to the Israelites: "On the fifteenth day of the seventh month the Lord's Feast of Tabernacles begins, and it lasts for seven days. The first day is a sacred assembly; do no regular work. For seven days present offerings made to the Lord by fire, and on the eighth day hold a sacred assembly and present an offering made to the Lord by fire. It is the closing assembly; do no regular work."'" [116]

The Feast Tabernacles is the last of the festivals and as such sums up all of the previous six. The festival year that began with Passover is now

---

[113] Leviticus 23:26-32
[114] Leviticus 16:17
[115] Kasdan, 79
[116] Leviticus 23:33-36

concluded with Sukkot. It is very special because it is the *seventh* festival, it begins in the *seventh* month, and lasts for *seven* days. It is a time for thanksgiving and celebration—a time, as Nehemiah said, to "enjoy choice food and sweet drink, and send some to those who have nothing prepared. This day is sacred to our Lord. Do not grieve, for the joy of the Lord is your strength." [117]

The Feast of Tabernacles also has a strong future aspect. Zechariah foretells a day when all nations will stream to Jerusalem to celebrate the Festival, and Revelation chapter 19 reveals its ultimate fulfillment in the Marriage Supper of the Lamb.

Past, Present and Future

All the festivals have a past, a present and a future aspect to them. They were given in the past as outworkings of the covenant relationship between God and Israel. They are a present reality in our yearly community life cycle as well as our daily lives. and they all will have a future fulfillment in the Kingdom of God.

Dan Juster, a Messianic Jewish rabbi and noted scholar writes: "I have come to see all the feasts as having great future prophetic reference awaiting fulfillment. Hence each feast has historic reference to God's salvation to ancient Israel, to the meaning of fulfillment in Yeshua [Jesus] who brings out the deepest meaning of the feast, to agricultural significance in celebrating God as the provider, and reference to the last days and the millennial age to come. [118]

The Pilgrimage Festivals

Of the seven feasts, three of them, Passover, Shavu'ot (Pentecost) and Sukkot (Tabernacles) are called Pilgrimage Festivals because they

---

[117] Nehemiah 8:10
[118] Juster, *Jewish Roots*, viii

required all the men in the land of Israel to appear before the Lord.[119] The Pilgrimage Festivals form the basis for this trilogy, as the three books feature these three festivals, respectively. In this section, they are discussed through the lens of Passover, as the primary festival.

The first appointed time is Passover, which first defined Israel as a nation in Exodus chapter 12. The command to celebrate Passover and begin the New Year with this observance was the first command given to the children of Israel. Thus their calling, mission and identity are bound up in Passover and the Passover-Exodus event.

Passover is the primary festival because it initiates the festival season and lends significance to all seven festivals. Further, it is an essential component of the three Pilgrimage Festivals. The Passover-Shavu'ot relationship is particularly strong because it is connected by the Counting of the Omer (the 50 days) and the journey from Exodus to Mt. Sinai. Thus Shavu'ot is called the *atzeret,* or "conclusion" of Passover. The journey that began in Egypt in the first month of the year brought the Israelites to Mt. Sinai in the third month.

This same relationship exists between Passover and Sukkot (The Feast of Tabernacles). In essence Sukkot draws its identity from Passover as well as from Shavu'ot, and fulfills and completes both of them. The three Pilgrimage Festivals are thus integral to one another and could be compared to the triune nature and revelation of the Godhead: the Son (Passover), the Spirit (Pentecost) and the Father (Tabernacles).

The centrality of Passover to the three Pilgrimage Festivals, the seven Levitical festivals, and indeed, to the redemptive master story of God in both the Old and New Testaments, is the rationale for naming this series The Passover Trilogy. While the second book is primarily about Pentecost, and the third book is primarily about the Feast of Tabernacles, these are rooted in, and surrounded by, the redemptive master-themes of Passover.

---

[119] Exodus 23:17, 34:23, Deuteronomy 16:16

Hebrew Terms

ADONAI (ah-doh-NAI): LORD. Used as a substitute for the name given to Moses at the burning bush.

Afikoman (ah-fee-KOH-men): "That which comes after" or "dessert" (actually a Greek word). On the Passover table is a plate with three *matzot* (plural for *matzah).* During the early part of the Seder the middle *matzah* is removed and broken in half. The larger half, now called the *Afikoman,* is wrapped in a white cloth and hidden. The child who finds it later is then rewarded.

Dayenu (die-AY-noo): "It would have been enough." Also the title of a song sung during the Seder. The song has fifteen verses which remind us of the fifteen songs of ascent, the fifteen steps leading up to the Temple and the fifteenth day of the month on which Passover occurs. It also reminds us of the fifteen steps in the Passover Seder.

Charoset (khah-ROH-set): A chopped-apple mixture with honey and nuts that reminds one of the mortar made for bricks in Egypt.

Hallel (hah-LEL): Psalms 113 to 118, which were chanted in the Temple while the Passover lambs were being slain.

Maror (mah-ROHR): Bitter herbs (often horseradish) representing the bitterness of slavery.

Matzah (MOTT-zah): Bread that has not risen and contains no yeast; unleavened bread. Plural: *Matzot.*

Mikveh (MICK-vuh): a ritual immersion basin, used by those seeking ceremonial purity. The Temple featured hundreds of these, allowing worshippers to fulfill the obligation of ritual cleanliness prior to entry. Plural: *mikva'ot*

Omer (OH-mare), **counting of**: The marking of the fifty days (seven weeks plus one) after Passover, leading to the celebration of *Shavuot*.

Seder (SAY-der): Literally, "order"; usually referring to the ceremonial Passover meal itself. There are many different Seder traditions.

Shavuot (shah-vu-OTE): The Feast of Weeks; a spring wheat-harvest festival that marks the end of the Counting of the *Omer*.

Sukkah (SOO-kuh): A small structure built as a temporary dwelling for the celebration of *Sukkot*. Observant Jews sleep in these at night, with a view of the stars, for the duration of the holiday.

Sukkot (soo-KOTE): The eight-day long Feast of Tabernacles; the seventh of God's appointed times as outlined in Leviticus 23. Some experts have concluded that Jesus was born during *Sukkot*.

Torah (TORE-ah): "Law". The first five books of the Bible. Also known as the "Law of Moses" or the Pentateuch.

Yeshua (yeh-SHOO-ah): Jesus' Hebrew name; what his relatives and peers would have called him. Literally, "Salvation" or "God Saves."

Key Passover Scriptures

Tree of Life Version

From the Torah

The Passover is mentioned in every book of the Torah except Genesis, underscoring its centrality to the idea of God's covenant with Israel. Excerpted below is the full account of the first Passover in Egypt, followed by brief passages from Numbers, Leviticus and Deuteronomy. The reader is encouraged to look up these passages to explore their context more fully.

Exodus 12:1-14

Now ADONAI spoke to Moses and Aaron in the land of Egypt saying, "This month will mark the beginning of months for you; it is to be the first month of the year for you. Tell all the congregation of Israel that on the tenth day of this month, each man is to take a lamb for his family, one lamb for the household. But if the household is too small for a lamb, then he and his nearest neighbor are to take one according to the number of the people. According to each person eating, you are to make your count for the lamb. Your lamb is to be without blemish, a year old male. You may take it from the sheep or from the goats. You must watch over it until the fourteenth day of the same month. Then the whole assembly of the congregation of Israel is to slaughter it at twilight. They are to take the blood and put it on the two doorposts and on the crossbeam of the houses where they will eat

it. They are to eat the meat that night, roasted over a fire.
With *matzot* and bitter herbs they are to eat it. Do not eat any of it
raw or boiled with water, but only roasted with fire—its head with its
legs and its innards. So let nothing of it remain until the morning.
Whatever remains until the morning you are to burn with fire. Also
you are to eat it this way: with your loins girded, your shoes on your
feet and your staff in your hand. You are to eat it in haste. It
is ADONAI's Passover.

For I will go through the land of Egypt on that night and strike
down every firstborn, both men and animals, and I will execute
judgments against all the gods of Egypt. I am ADONAI. The blood will
be a sign for you on the houses where you are. When I see the blood, I
will pass over you. So there will be no plague among you to destroy
you when I strike the land of Egypt. This day is to be a memorial for
you. You are to keep it as a feast to ADONAI. Throughout your
generations you are to keep it as an eternal ordinance.

Leviticus 23:5

During the first month, on the fourteenth day of the month in the
evening, is ADONAI's Passover.

Numbers 28:16-17

On the fourteenth day of the first month is ADONAI's Passover. On
the fifteenth day, there is to be a feast. For seven days, *matzot* will be
eaten.

Deuteronomy 16:1-3

Observe the month of *Aviv* [120] and keep the Passover to ADONAI

---

[120] The first month of the Hebrew calendar

your God, for in the month of *Aviv* ADONAI your God brought you out from Egypt by night. You are to sacrifice the Passover offering to ADONAI your God, from the flock and the herd, in the place ADONAI chooses to make His Name dwell. You are not to eat *hametz* [121] with it. For seven days you are to eat *matzot* with it, the bread of affliction—for you came out from the land of Egypt in haste. Do this so that all the days of your life you will remember the day when you came out from the land of Egypt.

From the Gospels

The account of Jesus leading his disciples in his final celebration of Passover is found in all three synoptic gospels. (Matthew 26:17-30, Mark 14:12-26, Luke 22:1-30) An excerpt from Mark's account is included below.

Mark 14:12-16, 22-26

Now on the first day of *matzah,* when they were slaughtering the Passover lamb, Yeshua's disciples said to Him, "Where do You want us to go and prepare for You to eat the Passover?"

He sent two of His disciples and told them, "Go into the city, and a man carrying a jar of water will meet you. Follow him, and wherever he enters, tell the homeowner, 'The Teacher says, "Where is My guest room, where I may eat the Passover with My disciples?"' He will show you a large upper room, furnished and ready. Make preparations for us there."

The disciples went out, came to the city, and found just what Yeshua had told them. And they prepared the Passover ...

---

[121] Yeast, or leaven

And while they were eating, He took the *matzah;* and after He offered the *bracha,* [122] He broke it and gave it to them and said, "Take; this is My body." And He took a cup; and after giving thanks, He gave to them and they all drank from it. And He said to them, "This is My blood of the covenant, which is poured out for many. Amen, I tell you, I will never again drink of the fruit of the vine, until that day when I drink it anew in the kingdom of God."

After singing the *Hallel,* they went out to the Mount of Olives.

---

[122] blessing

Resources

Bibliography and Recommended Books

Bailey, Kenneth E. *Jesus Through Middle Eastern Eyes: Cultural Studies in the Gospels.* Downers Grove: IVP Academic, 2008.

Beale, G.K. and D.A. Carson, ed. *Commentary on the New Testament use of the Old Testament.* Grand Rapids: Baker Academic, 2007.

Edersheim, Alfred. *Sketches of Jewish Social Life.* Peabody: Hendrickson Publishers, 1994.

Edersheim, Alfred. *The Life and Times of Jesus the Messiah.* Peabody: Hendrickson Publishers, 1886.

Edersheim, Alfred. *The Temple: Its Ministry and Services As They Were at the Time of Jesus Christ.* Grand Rapids: Eerdmans, 1992.

Finto, Don. *Your People Shall Be My People: Expanded Edition.* Chosen Books, 2016.

Hagner, Donald A. *The Jewish Reclamation of Jesus: An Analysis and Critique of the Modern Jewish Study of Jesus.* Grand Rapids: Zondervan, 1984.

Hoppin, Ruth. *Priscilla's Letter: Finding the Author of the Epistle to the Hebrews.* Fort Bragg, California: Lost Coast Press, 2000.

Jeremias, Joachim. *Jerusalem in the Time of Jesus.* Philadelphia: Fortress Press, 1962.

Juster, Dan. *Jewish Roots: Understanding Your Jewish Faith.*
Gaithersburg: Davar Publishing, 2013.

Kaiser, Walter C. Jr. *Mission in the Old Testament: Israel as a Light to the Nations.* Grand Rapids: Baker Academic, 2000.

Kasdan, Barney. *God's Appointed Times.* Clarksville: Messianic Jewish Publishers, 1993.

Keener, Craig S. *The Historical Jesus of the Gospels.* Grand Rapids: Eerdmans, 2009.

Keener, Craig S. *The IVP Bible Background Commentary: New Testament.* Grand Rapids: Eerdmans, 1993.

Keener, Craig S. *Romans: A New Covenant Commentary.* Eugene: Cascade: 2009.

Lapide, Pinchas. *The Resurrection of Jesus: a Jewish Perspective.* Minneapolis: Augsburg, 1983.

Lightfoot, John. *A Commentary on the New Testament from the Talmud and Hebraica: Volume 4.* Peabody: Hendrickson Publishers, 1979.

Rosen, Moishe and Ceil Rosen. *Christ in the Passover.* Chicago: Moody Press, 2006.

Sarna, Nahum M. "Exodus" *The JPS Torah Commentary,* edited by Nahum M. Sarna and Chaim Potok. Jerusalem: The Jewish Publication Society, 1989.

Seif, Jeffrey L. "Yeshua and Israel in the Third Millennium." The King's University, 2011.

Skarsaune, Oskar. *In the Shadow of the Temple.* Downers Grove: InterVarsity Press, 2002.

Stein, Robert H. *The Method and Message of Jesus' Teaching.*

Philadelphia: The Westminster Press, 1978.

Stern, David H. *Complete Jewish Bible.* Clarksville: Jewish New
Testament Publications, 1998.

Stern, David H. *Jewish New Testament Commentary.* Clarksville:
Jewish New Testament Publications, 1992.

Stern, David H. *Messianic Judaism: A Modern Movement With an
Ancient Past.* Clarksville: Jewish New Testament Publications,
2013.

Vermes, Geza. *The Resurrection.* New York: Doubleday, 2008.

Wilson, Marvin. *Our Father Abraham: Jewish Roots of the Christian
Faith.* Grand Rapids: Eerdmans, 1989.

Books by Jim Jacob

To learn more about Jesus as the Jewish Messiah, we recommend
three books by Jim Jacob. You can read them for free online at
www.jimjacobbooks.com/read-for-free, or purchase a printed copy.

A Lawyer's Case for the Resurrection offers historical and logical
evidence for the Resurrection of Jesus, including documentation from
Jewish sources and others who do not believe Jesus was the Messiah.

A Lawyer's Case for God offers evidence for the existence of God and
the validity of the Bible. It also addresses topics such as: the problem
with organized religion, the myth of being a "good person", that the
idea that Jews don't believe in Jesus, and whether the Bible is, in fact,
outdated.

A Lawyer's Case for His Faith builds on *A Lawyer's Case for God* and also explores topics such as: the existence of a good God in a world filled with suffering, the notion that all religions can be correct, whether the bible and science can be reconciled, and the identity of Jesus as the Jewish Messiah.

Bibles & Commentaries

Complete Jewish Bible (CJB). Clarksville: Jewish New Testament Publications, 1998.

Stern, David H. *Jewish New Testament Commentary*. Clarksville: Jewish New Testament Publications, 1992.

The Holy Bible, *Tree of Life Version (TLV)*. Grand Rapids: Baker Books, 2015.

Haggadot [123]

Fleischer, David. *What Makes this Night Different from all other Nights? A Messianic Haggadah for Pesach*. San Francisco: Congregation B'nai Brit HaMashiah, 1997.

Rubin, Barry and Steffi Rubin. *The Messianic Passover Haggadah*. Clarksville: Messianic Jewish Publishers, 2005.

Websites

OurFatherAbraham.com – Devoted to the purpose of educating followers and admirers of Jesus about the Hebraic context of the good news, and the centrality of the Jewish festivals to the Christian faith.

---

[123] Passover Seder Handbooks. The word means "telling". Hebrew singular: *haggadah*.

MessianicJewish.net – Reaching out to Jewish people with the message of Messiah and teaching our non-Jewish spiritual family about their Jewish roots.

Hebrew4Christians.com – An excellent resource for those interested in Hebrew. The vision is to provide a resource for the Church regarding its rich Hebraic heritage by promoting Jewish literacy among all those who believe in Jesus.

Primary Messianic Organizations

There are many Messianic Jewish and Messianic Gentile organizations (non-profit and congregational). Following are several of the primary organizations along with their vision statements, according to their websites.

Tikkun International (www.tikkunministries.org) – Tikkun International is a Messianic Jewish umbrella organization for an apostolic network of leaders, congregations and ministries in covenantal relationship for mutual accountability, support and equipping to extend the Kingdom of God in America, Israel, and throughout the world.

Messianic Jewish Alliance of America (www.mjaa.org) – Founded in 1915, the MJAA is the largest association of Messianic Jewish and non-Jewish believers in Yeshua (Hebrew for Jesus) in the world. Its purpose is threefold: (1) to testify to the large and growing number of Jewish people who believe that Yeshua is the promised Jewish Messiah and Savior of the world, (2) to bring together Jewish and non-Jewish people who have a shared vision for Jewish revival, and, most importantly (3) to introduce their Jewish brothers and sisters to the Jewish Messiah Yeshua.

International Alliance of Messianic Congregations and Synagogues (www.iamcs.org) – The spiritual vision of the IAMCS is to see the outpouring of God's Spirit upon Jewish people through Messianic congregations. The IAMCS is not designed to be a denominational structure, but rather to be an instrument in promoting Messianic revival and to provide for the needs of its members, whatever their affiliations.

Union of Messianic Jewish Congregations (www.umjc.org) – The UMJC is a network of over 75 congregations in 8 countries. Together, they establish and grow Jewish congregations that honor Yeshua, the Messiah of Israel. For nearly 40 years, the Union has provided a venue for mutual support, lively debate, joint activism, and practical leadership development.

About the Authors

Lon A. Wiksell, D.Min.

Originally from Sioux City, Iowa, Lon grew up in church as the son of Pentecostal pastors. He completed his first two years of college in Iowa before moving to Springfield Missouri and working for Evangel University where he met his wife Fran. He later worked for Drury University and Missouri State University, where he also completed his BS and MBA. After working for Phillips Petroleum Company in Bartlesville, Oklahoma he moved the family to Tulsa in 1988, to study at Oral Roberts University. He received his M.Div. from there in 1992. After graduating they moved to Kansas City where they became involved in the Messianic Jewish movement. In 2013 he received his Doctorate of Ministry in Messianic Jewish Studies from The King's University.

Lon and Fran were co-founders and co-leaders of Or HaOlam Messianic Congregation from 1995 to 2002. They then went on to start House of Messiah in 2004, devoted to understanding the words of Yeshua (Jesus) within their historical context and celebrating the biblical festivals as a pattern of personal and community life. House of Messiah has now merged with Kingdom Living Messianic Congregation, and Lon and Fran are now highly involved in organizing city-wide biblical festivals.

Ryan Wiksell

Ryan was raised in the Assemblies of God in Northeastern Oklahoma, and joined the Messianic Jewish movement with his family in Kansas City during his high school years. A personal call to ministry then led him to study music and theology at Evangel University.

Doors were then opened for him to serve in various Southern Baptist churches, where he held positions in music leadership and communications. Ryan married Christina in 2003, and shortly thereafter they pursued a call to plant a grassroots independent church in downtown Springfield, MO, called The Front Porch. After this effort drew to a close in 2011, they sought out a new spiritual family, which they found in Christ Episcopal Church in Springfield.

Today, Ryan and Christina are blessed to be the parents of twin four-year-olds Asher and Anya. Ryan and his family are currently residing in Alexandria, Virginia, while he is enrolled in the Master of Divinity program at Virginia Theological Seminary.